Jaguin's Love:
Dragon Lords of Valdier Book 8

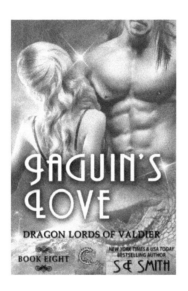

By S. E. Smith

Acknowledgments

I would like to thank my husband Steve for believing in me and being proud enough of me to give me the courage to follow my dream. I would also like to give a special thank-you to Sally, Debbie, Julie, Jolanda and Narelle, who listen to me, read my stories, and encourage me to be me.

—S. E. Smith

Montana Publishing
Science Fiction Romance
JAGUIN'S LOVE: DRAGON LORDS OF VALDIER
BOOK 8
Copyright © 2016 by Susan E. Smith
First E-Book Published June 2016
Cover Design by Melody Simmons

Summary: An alien warrior discovers his mate close to death and will do whatever it takes to heal her, even if it means setting her free.

ISBN: 978-1-942562-93-1 (Paperback)
ISBN: 978-1-942562-94-8 (eBook)

Published in the United States by Montana Publishing.

{1. Science Fiction Romance. – Fiction. 2. Science Fiction – Fiction. 3. Paranormal – Fiction. 4. Romance – Fiction.}

www.montanapublishinghouse.com

Synopsis

Jaguin is one of the finest trackers on Valdier. To date, there is only one thing he has never been successful at finding – his true mate. That failure is eating away at him and his dragon. Even his symbiot is feeling the drain as the centuries crawl by with no end to the emptiness gnawing away at them. Hope flares with the discovery of a species that is compatible with their own. The Lords of Valdier have found their true mates on a distant planet, bringing hope to the warriors of Valdier where females are few and true mates almost non-existent.

Jaguin is rewarded for his help in tracking one of the Lord's stubborn females with the promise of a chance to find his own true mate on the planet called Earth. His search appears fruitless until the last mission before they are to leave.

Sara Wilson is a botanist working with the National University of Colombia. Her love of plants and their potential for medicinal uses consume her life. She feels confident she is on the verge of a breakthrough when she is kidnapped by a cartel boss with only one thing on his mind – to exact revenge. A revenge that not only comes close to taking her life, but will change it forever.

After a fruitless search for his mate, Jaguin accepts one last assignment to guard Lord Creon's mate, Carmen, during a mission to seek justice against the man who brutally murdered her husband back on Earth. Instead, he finds his true mate in the man's cruel clutches, barely clinging to life. His only thought is to spirit her away where he and his symbiot can heal her and his dragon can claim her.

The scars left during her captivity run deep inside Sara as she struggles to come to terms with her new life. She is no longer on Earth, but the fear and terror still haunt her.

She needs time to discover who she is again and whether this is a life she can accept.

Can Jaguin's love heal the scars on the inside or will his true mate believe she has traded one monster for another?

Table of Contents

Chapter 1

With growing apprehension, Jaguin moved down the long interior corridor of the building he and his companions had just entered. His gaze swept warily over the area, searching for danger. This mission was supposed to be simple: protect Prince Creon's mate, Carmen Walker-Reykill. The trouble was that there was never anything simple when it came to the unusual human female. Personally, he would have felt much better if Creon had simply tied Carmen up and left her on board the spaceship or back at the ranch belonging to their human ally, Paul Grove.

Pushing down the feeling, he once more scanned the interior walls of Javier Cuello's house, searching for any type of detection equipment, or weapons, that might warn the human that they were there.

There was nothing but polished dark wood and off-white walls. A few paintings hung to brighten the décor, but that was all as far as he could tell.

The human male they were seeking was ridiculously overconfident, believing the few men he had hired would protect him. It might have worked – against other humans – but the number of soldiers patrolling the area or stationed in the tall towers outside were no match against Jaguin, Gunner, Creon, and their symbiots.

They were not from this world, but from Valdier, an alien world light-years away. The Valdier were a dragon-shifting species known in their star system for their fierceness in battle. It did not take them long to take care of the men outside before moving to the interior of Javier Cuello's home.

Each Valdier warrior was made up of not one, but three components that made him a deadly force against their enemies. The first component was the man, the secondary form was his dragon, and the third component was his symbiot. They worked as a team to overcome any threat. It was the Goddess' way of balancing them. Their curse was that all three needed to accept a female if she was to be their true mate.

An almost impossible task given how hard-headed and picky my symbiot and dragon are, he thought with a sigh of resignation and acceptance.

Jaguin's gaze moved once more to the female beside him. A wave of envy swept through him for a moment. He and many others on Valdier had given up hope of ever finding their true mates. Unmated females on Valdier had grown fewer and fewer over the centuries, leaving most warriors with a growing feeling of despair that they would never find a mate. Without one, their dragon's need to mate would drive them mad. They could only hope to die in battle before that occurred. Jaguin understood those feelings and the growing concern all too well.

The fact that he was having difficulty controlling his dragon at this moment proved he was nearing the time when he would have to return to his home in the mountains. He would have to admit to the elders that his time had come to move on to the next life.

Jaguin had hoped to find a true mate among the humans, just as Creon and his brothers had. He had searched for the last few weeks, but none of the females he had seen from a distance stirred the dragon in him or excited his symbiot. It was time to admit that it was not his destiny to find a mate in this lifetime.

This was not the Valdier's first trip to this planet, though it was for him. Zoran Reykill, the leader of the Valdier, had discovered this strange, beautiful world after escaping captivity from a traitorous group of individuals intent on restarting the war between the Valdier, Curizan, and Sarafin. The next trip was to retrieve Paul Grove, the father of Kelan Reykill's true mate. This trip was different, though. This time they were on Earth so that Carmen Reykill could find closure against the man who had killed her previous mate and unborn child.

Jaguin understood Carmen's need for revenge. He also knew the dangers involved in such a mission. Emotions often ran high in situations such as this and they could lead to deadly mistakes. It was Jaguin's and Gunner's responsibility to make sure that nothing happened to Carmen. If she died, then so would their prince. No one survived the death of their true mate.

What made it even more challenging was the fact that Carmen was obviously pregnant. The man in him wanted to protect her, while the dragon wanted to lock her in a padded room where nothing could touch her.

The wave of unease flowing through him increased, clawing at his insides like his dragon shredding the flesh of his prey. He could feel both his symbiot and his dragon pushing against him. Something was wrong. He felt the sensation growing the closer they got to the compound. Scales rippled over his skin beneath the cover of his shirt, a visible sign of his dragon's agitation.

Something not right, his dragon suddenly growled inside of him. *I smell blood.*

Jaguin could almost taste the coppery-scent in the air. Concerned, he shot a sharp glance to Creon Reykill. Creon returned his wary look with a barely perceptible nod. He smelled it as well.

Jaguin felt his symbiot's agitation as it moved beside him. Its body shimmered, reflecting the colors of the hallway, and it continually shifted from one form to another as if it wasn't sure what to expect. That in itself heightened Jaguin's concern for the delicate yet fierce female between himself and Gunner.

"I don't like this," Gunner mumbled under his breath. "Creon, I think one of us should escort Lady Carmen out of here."

"No," Carmen hissed, staring at the door at the end of the corridor that a young human female had silently pointed to when they entered the building. "I have to finish this."

"Stay close," Creon growled under his breath. "Remember your promise to me, Carmen."

Jaguin saw Carmen's gaze soften for a moment when she turned to look at Creon. "I will. I promise," she whispered.

"At the first sign of danger, get her out of here," Creon muttered to him before turning back toward the door. "Open it!" He ordered with a wave of his hand to his symbiot.

In a flash, the golden body shot forward, bursting through the thick double doors at the end of the corridor. The symbiot's body shifted, forming long tentacles that reached out and wrapped around the men inside the room. Jaguin moved forward to cover Carmen's body with his own while Gunner took the position behind her.

The first thing that struck Jaguin when they entered was the overwhelming smell of blood. His symbiot surged past him and he felt a sharp pain lance through his body at its distress. The intensity of it left him stunned and he actually stumbled a step before recovering. His gaze swept the room before it froze in horror on the figure hanging limply from a roughly constructed frame. The body of the slender human female was covered in blood. Her head was bent forward, allowing the long, thick braid of blonde hair to partially conceal her face. Her arms were stretched at a painful angle, supporting her body and making the torture that much worse.

A suffocating rage struck him hard followed by an intense wave of unexpected grief. Shock held him motionless for a moment. The rage he could understand... but the grief? He drew in a shaky breath when his symbiot turned to him. He could feel its plea for help. His dragon strained to get to the woman. In that moment, he understood their powerful reaction. He had finally found the one thing he had spent centuries searching for.

Our mate! His dragon roared in grief.

* * *

Sara Wilson clung to the small thread of life like a starving dog to a bone. She had passed beyond pain, her mind in a dazed fog. She knew enough about the human body to know that her body wasn't ready to give up yet. Her heart was still young and strong. It was her spirit that was slowly fading.

She was barely conscious. A part of her was afraid to give in to the darkness clouding the corners of her vision. She was afraid if she did, she might never wake up again. She wanted to live, despite what was happening to her.

Her arms ached from holding her weight. There was nothing she could do about it; her legs refused to support her any longer. A part of her wished she had been a little more vocal when she called the men in the room sick cowards who didn't have the balls to face her one at a time. The sane part of her brain chided her for provoking them in the first place.

Emma had warned her. The younger girl had given Sara broken and tortured words of caution not to fight against the men.

"They'll kill you like they did the other girl," Emma had whispered. "They'll beat you and let you heal before they beat you again. Don't fight them. They killed her when she fought back."

Emma had grown quiet after that, refusing to talk. Sara understood why now. This was Sara's second session with the insane bastards. The first session, she had listened to Emma and kept her mouth shut.

They had laughed when they beat her the first time. Her face, arms, and torso still showed the marks of that beating. As Cuello struck her, he had called her by another woman's name – Carmen, Carmen Walker. Sara didn't know who the woman was, she just hoped to hell that the bastard never found her. The hatred in his gaze, his words, in his every action made it easy to understand that he wanted to kill Carmen. She and Emma were, unfortunately, a poor substitute.

Sara had tried to keep quiet when their guard shoved them into the room, she really did, at least until she had seen what they were planning. The guard had grabbed Emma first. Sara couldn't stand the thought of the younger, more delicate woman being whipped. She'd fought – and lost.

Sara had cursed them, struggling to break free of the bonds. When the first licks of the whip had slashed across her flesh, she'd screamed, but she had sealed her lips together after realizing that the more she cried out, the more Cuello laughed.

Her silence had infuriated the man, but no matter what he did, she had kept quiet, using every bit of her astounding level of stubbornness.

Sara had cultivated that particular characteristic during a childhood surrounded by ten male 'cousins' – only half of which were actually related to her – in a home from hell. Her mom had been young when she had Sara. It'd been easier to dump Sara on her older sister and pretend that the birth never happened.

Her aunt had five boys of her own, but being a foster mom had earned her extra cash. The only girl, Sara, had been shuffled to the attic of the old farmhouse along with all the discards and forgotten pieces of junk.

Sara had learned two important things during her time in the hills of the Appalachian Mountains: stay outside as much as possible and never show your fear. She'd grown up fighting for leftovers at the dinner table, among other things.

When some of the boys, two of which were related by blood, had thought it'd be fun to play doctor, Sara had learned to fight with her fists, feet, and anything else she could use.

When she complained to her aunt and uncle, they had both called her a troublemaker looking for attention, and had marched her up to the attic to think about her wicked ways. Sara had snuck out of the window and climbed down the old water tower next to the house.

When she was sixteen, Sara left and never looked back. A teacher during her tenth year at school had introduced her to the freedom she could have if she focused on her education. Sara did that, not stopping until she reached her dream of independence.

She achieved a Doctorate in Herbal Medicine and Botany. That was the only good thing to come of her childhood – the time she'd spent around plants, cultivating a fascination for what they were and what they could be used for.

Sara didn't know what had stopped the agonizing torture, but she was thankful. The sound of an explosion pulled her back from the brink of oblivion. She tried to raise her head, but it took more energy than she had left inside her. Instead, she vaguely hoped that it was the Colombian army invading to stop Cuello. She doubted that was the case, but a detached part of her brain held to the stubborn wish.

The soft sound of claws against the polished wood caught her attention. Forcing her eyelids to open, she thought she saw a flash of gold. A barely audible moan escaped her as she sagged, causing even more of a strain on her already stretched arms.

"Cut her down," a voice said behind her.

The stubborn hope flared once again. Her session was over. She only hoped that didn't mean it was Emma's turn. Fear rose inside her and she weakly struggled against the restraints.

"No," she protested, her voice a faint thread of sound.

"You're alive!" A husky male voice responded.

Another moan escaped Sara as her wrists were suddenly freed and she fell into hard, muscular arms.

Something soft and warm moved over her skin and covered her shredded back. Almost immediately, the pain dissolved.

"Don't...," she forced out, unable to open her eyes to look at the man holding her.

"Don't what, my mate?" The voice whispered.

Sara's foggy brain heard the words, but couldn't comprehend them. It was taking everything inside her to remain conscious despite the soothing feeling along her back. Whatever they had decided to place on it was taking all the pain, burning, and stinging away. She wondered if it was a type of plant found locally.

"Don't... hurt Emma," she finally finished, forcing her tired brain back to her current situation. "I... can take... it."

A warm, soothing hand ran down along her face, brushing the loose strands of hair back. She wanted to turn her cheek into it. Fear pulled at her. What if this was another trick? What if they wanted her to think they were stopping only to start all over again? Her mind shattered at the thought and she released the slender hold she had on her consciousness.

Warmth surrounded her as she fell into the inky darkness. For the first time in her life, for a few brief seconds, Sara felt safe, protected. Then she let go and everything went blissfully silent.

"Never, my fierce flower, never again," the voice said.

Sara didn't hear the words. If she had, she would have been even more frightened at the hard edge to them. It wasn't directed at her, but for her. It was a promise of things to come.

Chapter 2

Jaguin paced outside of the sick bay. His symbiot remained inside with the healer, working to save their mate. He had wanted to stay, but Tandor, the ship's chief medical officer, had kicked him out, telling Jaguin that his symbiot was helpful but Jaguin was just getting in his way. It would take both of them to keep the female alive.

Turning, he walked ten paces to the left before swiveling on his heel to retrace his steps. He kept the door to the medical unit within his sight at all times. His fingers automatically went to the golden cuff on his forearm every few seconds as he impatiently waited.

"How is she?" He demanded in a husky voice, stroking the golden living metal.

Images of the woman suddenly appeared in his mind. She was lying on her side. Her back was covered with a thin layer of his symbiot's gold body as it worked on healing her. The layer dissolved and he could see the thick ridges of sealed, red flesh before it was covered with another layer. The healer was working on her other injuries.

Pain, anger, and grief poured through him. He raised his head when he heard the sound of footsteps. He watched as Gunner walked down the corridor toward him. His friend's lips were pressed into a thin line.

"How is she?" Gunner asked as he came to a stop next to him.

"Alive… barely," Jaguin replied, dropping his hand from the symbiot band on his arm.

"What of the other female?" Gunner asked with a heavy sigh of relief.

Jaguin shook his head. "I don't know," he admitted. "I have focused only on the one I brought on board."

"It is understandable. She was the one with the worst injuries," Gunner responded with a tired sigh. "I do not understand the human males. How can they treat something so precious, so fragile, like this?"

"I don't know," Jaguin said again, leaning back against the wall. "Where did you get that bruise? I don't remember seeing it before."

Gunner reached up and rubbed his jaw, wincing when he touched the sensitive spot on the right side. The wound looked new. A mischievous gleam lit Gunner's eyes.

"From the precious, delicate human female that I brought back. I tried to steal a kiss," he chuckled with a shrug. "Audrey dared me to try. How could I resist such a challenge? For a healer and a female, she can hit very hard. I will listen to her when she warns me next time."

Jaguin shook his head and a reluctant smile curved his lips before it faded and an intense look came into his eyes. His gaze moved back to the door of the medical unit. The memories of his mate's words haunted him.

"The female is my mate," he stated in a husky voice.

"What?!" Gunner's shocked tone ricocheted through him. "Are you sure?"

"Yes," Jaguin replied in a soft voice. "My symbiot is with her. My dragon is on edge, just as I am. It is... difficult not to be with her."

Gunner rubbed the red spot on his chin and grimaced. "Yes, it is," he muttered, straightening along with Jaguin when the door to the medical unit opened.

"Is she...?" Jaguin started to ask before his throat tightened. He drew in a deep breath before he continued. "How is she?"

Tandor's expression was grim when he nodded to both men. Jaguin watched as Tandor ran his hand tiredly down his face and rubbed his chin before his hand dropped to his side. He motioned for Jaguin and Gunner to follow him into the medical unit.

Jaguin started forward, his gaze automatically moving to the woman lying silently on the bed. He could see the thick bands of living gold on her neck and wrists. His symbiot sat on the far side of the bed resting its head on the pristine white sheets. Small threads of gold wove outward from it, replacing the narrow ribbons still moving over her body.

"It is a good thing you are her mate," Tandor replied in a quiet voice, walking past the two beds toward the office area to the left. "She would not have survived without your symbiot's ability to heal her. Our medical advancements are far greater than most, but nothing can heal the body the way a symbiot can."

"What of the other woman?" Gunner asked with a frown. "She is not mated."

"She had a concussion, as well as other injuries," Tandor admitted with a shake of his head. "I was able to heal most, but not even our symbiots can heal a broken mind or soul. The female was awake, but she never spoke or responded. It was as if only her body was here, nothing else. I can see the injuries inflicted to the females on a physical level, but can only guess at the damage done on a mental one. Time will tell if they will survive."

"This one has to," Jaguin retorted, turning to glance again through the clear glass where his mate lay. "She… She is mine."

Tandor's gaze followed Jaguin's to the peaceful face. "I know," he murmured. "You will need to be patient, Jaguin. Until she wakes, I can only guess at the damage that was done to her mind."

Jaguin's gaze remained locked on the young woman's face. He didn't even know her name. She looked like a pale statue. Her breathing was so slight that he could barely see her chest rise and fall. His symbiot moved closer, nudging one slender arm.

Hope and determination flared inside him when her arm slid over the golden head. He knew that it was the nudge of his symbiot that caused her arm to move, but not her fingers. Warmth flooded him when the woman's fingers curled ever so slightly into the silky smooth body of his symbiot.

"I will wait however long it takes," Jaguin replied, the promise resonating deep within him.

* * *

Sara was locked in the nightmare of her memories again. A small part of her brain was telling her that it was only a memory, not real, but she swore she could feel the ripping of her flesh with each slash of the whip. Her jaw locked so tightly that her teeth ached, but she refused to give Cuello the satisfaction of hearing her scream.

Her body stiffened in surprise when a wave of warmth suddenly engulfed her. It was a golden flood of liquid, washing away the pain and soothing her. For a moment, she couldn't catch her breath. It was as if she were being torn apart. One part of her was locked in the horror of her captivity, while the other part was free as another world rose up to surround her.

Confusion swamped her as the vivid images exploded in her mind. She expected the memory to take her to a time either when she was a child or back in Columbia when she was working at the university there. Instead, the world was strange, different, in a good way, from anything she had ever seen before.

Her fingers involuntarily spread as she reached for the tall grass. It was purple! She had never seen grass like this before. Her hand brushed over the tops. Her lips curved upward as it tickled her palm. The faint smile turned to a frown when another wave of warmth filled her.

What is going on? Am I dead? She wondered, gazing around the meadow.

No, elila, you are not dead, merely sleeping, a husky voice responded.

As she tried to take everything in, her heart pounded so hard that she thought it would explode. The faint sound of a soft murmur brushed over her a moment before she felt something cold against her neck. Within seconds, her body relaxed. Whatever she was given was pulling her deeper into the vast pit that she had unwittingly stumbled into.

I'll hide here, she thought as her body landed in a soft bed of gold. *He'll never find me in the dark.*

Chapter 3

Three days later, Sara moaned softly. She forced her eyelids to open a crack. Her fingers curled into the covers. She was surprised at their softness. Cautiously, she opened her eyes a bit more so that she could get a better look at where she was.

When she turned her head, she saw Emma sitting in a chair in the corner. The younger girl looked even paler and more fragile than before. Sara shoved her own feelings of weakness aside and pushed up until she was in a sitting position. A soft growl of annoyance escaped her when her arms trembled.

"Damn it," she muttered, lifting a shaky hand to brush her hair back from her face.

Sara's hand froze in surprise when she realized that while she might be weak as a kitten, she wasn't in pain. A confused frown creased her brow. How long had it been since Cuello had her strapped to that horrible wooden frame?

She slowly lowered her hand and gazed around the room. It was stark in some ways, almost futuristic. On the other side of a clear panel, there was a wide door that looked like it might lead out to another room. There were two beds in the room she was in and several chairs that looked comfortable.

Her gaze moved back to Emma. Worry pulled at Sara when she saw the haunted look in Emma's eyes. Pushing the thin sheet covering her legs to the side, Sara paused for a moment. There were no bruises marring her skin. She rolled her shoulders and waited for the pain, but none came.

Emma's eyes cleared for a moment and she silently shook her head. The look in them didn't reassure Sara. Instead of relief, a look of terror flashed through her eyes before they glazed over again and turned dull. Sara could almost feel Emma pulling away from the world.

Sara tightened her jaw in determination. She hadn't spend half her life fighting for her freedom just to kiss it goodbye. Her gaze flashed past Emma to the doors before they moved to the office. She could see that the door to it was open. Maybe, just maybe, whoever it belonged to had left a weapon of some type inside.

Sara straightened and stiffened her spine. The first mistake the bastards made was to allow her to heal. She didn't know why they'd left her alone long enough for her to heal so completely, but she certainly wasn't going to trust that whoever it was that had them now was done with them. She and Emma would never be tortured ever again, Sara would make sure of that. The second mistake was leaving them alone. If there was a way out, Sara would find it, and whether Emma wanted to go or not, she wasn't leaving the other woman behind.

Turning back to Emma, Sara gave the other woman a look that used to send more than one of her cousins running for cover. When Sara decided she wanted something, nothing stopped her. This time, she wanted her freedom.

"Let's go," she ordered in a harder voice than she'd intended. "I need you here with me, Emma. We are going together or not at all, do you understand?"

Emma nodded and rose to her feet. Sara saw the younger woman sway, but there was also a quiet resolve when she pulled her shoulders back. Sara smiled and reached her hand out. Her fingers closed around Emma's hand and she gently squeezed it.

"We'll make it," Sara promised. "I won't let anything happen to you."

Emma's lips parted and she looked like she was about to say something before an overwhelming look of sadness darkened her eyes and she shook her head. Sara could tell the other woman was struggling to say something. It was almost as if Emma had forgotten how to speak. She was about to ask Emma what was wrong when the double doors slid open.

Sara's lips parted in surprise and shock when a huge golden creature trotted in, carrying something in its mouth. Her throat worked up and down when it suddenly stopped and dropped the soft fabric figure. Sara unconsciously pulled on Emma, tugging the other woman behind her when the creature tilted its head to the side and stared back at her.

Sara's right hand rose to her throat. Her fingers froze when she felt a delicate rope of metal hanging around it. The moment she touched it, a sense of déjà vu struck her, and the familiar wave of warmth flooded through her fingertips and down her arm.

"It was you…," she whispered.

Her eyes jerked upward when the shadowy figure of a large man suddenly darkened the entryway. Her eyes widened as recognition dawned on her. It was the man from the forest in her dream.

"No...!" Her angry cry echoed in the spartan room.

Her mind shattered, no longer seeing that she and Emma were not in the cells in Cuello's compound, just recognizing that they were once again captives. Her gaze flew around the room, searching for a weapon. Not seeing any, she clenched her fists and relaxed her shoulders.

"Emma, when I tell you to run, you run and don't look back," Sara hissed, her eyes narrowing on the man in front of her.

She could feel Emma's hand on her lower back tremble in response. All she could do was try to delay the man long enough for Emma to find a way to escape. Drawing in a deep breath, Sara started forward – only to be intercepted when the huge golden creature stepped in front of her, carrying in its mouth the object it had dropped earlier.

Sara paused in confusion when it raised its head and pushed the object toward her. Her gaze moved back and forth between the creature and the man. She wasn't sure what to do.

"My symbiot... It wishes for you to have this," the man said. "I searched for human objects that are given to the sick. This came up. My symbiot saw this as your favorite."

Sara didn't say anything; she just stared warily at the man. Her brain picked out words in his sentence that didn't make sense to her... symbiot... human object... sick...

"I wasn't sick, I was... beaten," Sara bit out in a husky voice.

"I know," the man replied in an accented voice that she couldn't place.

"Where are we?" Sara demanded, glancing up at him. She still couldn't see him very clearly with the dim light inside and the brilliant light of the corridor shadowing his face. "Are you with the military?"

The man hesitated before he responded. "You are on board the *Horizon*. You and the other female needed immediate medical attention. I am a warrior, one of the best trackers for my people."

"Cuello...," Sara started to say, stopping when the man took a slight step forward.

"The male and his companions are dead. You need never fear them again," the man replied in a calm, hard tone. "I would have preferred to have killed him myself, but Lady Carmen completed that task, as was her right."

Carmen..., Sara thought fuzzily. She started when the golden creature nudged her hand. She had forgotten all about it. A frown creased her brow and she trembled. She was fast losing the small amount of strength she'd had when she first woke. Between the beatings and lack of food, her body was running on empty.

"What is this thing?" She asked, staring down into the golden eyes. When it first came in, it had looked like some kind of huge cat. Now it looked like the sloth figurines that she loved to collect. "It was a cat a minute ago."

"Yes, it can change shape. It knows you like this creature and it wishes to calm you," the man said.

Sara's hands automatically reached out when the creature leaned toward her and dropped a fabric replica of a sloth. It fell into her outstretched palms. Tears burned her eyes when the creature slowly sank down until it was sitting and stared at her with wide, golden eyes. Her gaze lifted to the man again. This time the soft light shining down illuminated his face.

"Where… Who… are you?" Sara asked in a faint voice.

"You are aboard the Valdier Warship *Horizon*. I am Jaguin, a warrior from the east mountain region of Valdier. I am… your protector," he added, taking another step closer.

Sara could feel Emma's hand violently tremble. It was a reminder that she wasn't alone. Her body swayed as her mind tried to comprehend what the man was and wasn't saying. Her lips parted and her throat moved up and down. She tried several times before the words finally came out.

"What are you?" She whispered, staring at him with wide eyes. "What do you want with us?"

The man paused in front of her. She already knew the answer. There were no creatures on Earth like the golden one watching her intently. There were no human men that looked like the man standing in front of her. Unless she was in some strange movie set, something very, very strange had happened back at Cuello's compound, something that involved golden tentacles and bizarre lights.

"I am an alien," the man finally replied. "You are my mate."

Sara's eyes widened even further before the last of her strength dissolved. She knew she was done when the darkness that was pushing at her continued to grow. She felt Emma's hands wrap around her, but there was no way the other girl could hold Sara up.

"Oh, great," Sara forced out as her eyelids fluttered several times.

Once again, she felt the rush of warmth surround her. This time, it wasn't soft and soothing but hard and muscular. Her head rolled to the side and her cheek rested against the coarse material of the man's shirt.

Out of the frying pan..., Sara vaguely thought as the darkness consumed her.

Chapter 4

Jaguin rolled the small stuffed creature he had replicated for Sara nervously between his hands. He wasn't sure how to approach his mate. He'd always thought that when he met her they would instantly recognize each other and everything would be perfect. That was the way it had worked for his parents. At least, that's what his father had told him.

When Jaguin was a youngling, he had asked his father how he would know when he met his true mate.

His father's reply had been short and to the point. "I saw your mother, she saw me, and we knew. You don't have much choice. When your dragon and your symbiot want something, there's no use fighting it. They will make your life miserable if you do."

"But, what of mother? Did she feel the same?" Jaguin had innocently asked.

He remembered his father's grin. The more he thought about it, the more he realized he should have noticed that it had wavered a bit before he answered.

"Eventually," his father had replied.

Jaguin had always meant to ask his mother, but there just never seemed to be a good time to question her about it. He had listened to the other boys in the village, but their fathers had pretty much said the same thing. The few females his age had been closely guarded by their families, so it wasn't like he could have asked them.

"Jaguin," a soft voice called from behind him.

Jaguin turned and watched as a slender but very pregnant Carmen waddled down the corridor toward him. He glanced over, expecting to see either Cree or Calo with her. His eyebrow rose when he saw she was alone.

"Lady Carmen," Jaguin replied politely, cupping the stuffed sloth in his hand and pressing it to his side.

Carmen's gaze flickered to the stuffed animal and a smile curved her lips. Another wave of envy coursed through Jaguin. He couldn't wait until his mate smiled at him.

"How are the women?" She asked, glancing at the door to the medical unit.

"Tandor wants them to stay a few extra days. He is concerned about their mental health. The youngest still has not spoken, even to my mate. He thought a few extra days would allow them to get acclimated to the ship and what has happened to them," he explained.

"Has the other woman woken up?" Carmen asked with a concerned frown.

Jaguin nodded. "Yes, yesterday, but not for long," he admitted. "I am hoping that she is awake. I would like to know what her name is."

Carmen's gaze softened when she saw his uneasy smile. "Would you mind if I went with you?" She asked in a slightly husky tone.

"No," Jaguin replied, stepping to the side. "It may calm the females to see another human of their gender."

Carmen chuckled. "Yes, it might," she agreed, stepping around him to the door.

Jaguin followed Carmen into the room. He was surprised to see Emma sitting on the bed. His gaze immediately went to the woman behind her. Sara was brushing Emma's hair with slow, steady strokes. There was a soft glow to her face that had been missing the day before. Her hand faltered when she saw him enter behind Carmen.

"Hello," Carmen greeted, walking toward the bed.

Sara's gaze jerked from his face back to Carmen. A confused frown creased her brow as she stared at Creon's mate. It was like she was trying to figure out if she was real, an alien like him, or a figment of her imagination. Jaguin realized at that moment that his mate had very expressive eyes. He quickly stored that information.

"Hello," Sara replied in a slower, uneasy voice.

Jaguin quickly reached for one of the chairs in the corner and carried it over to set it next to the bed. He watched Sara with a heated gaze as she glanced back at him before her gaze settled on the stuffed sloth.

"This is for you," he quickly muttered, holding it out to her. "It is slightly different from the other one. I discovered that there is more than one type of this creature on your world."

A soft giggle escaped the younger woman before she dropped her gaze to the bed. It took a moment for his mate to reach for it. He stepped back and glanced toward the office where Tandor was watching him with an amused grin on his face. Jaguin scowled at the healer.

"I'll leave you alone for a few moments," he said with a slight scowl. "I will speak with Tandor."

Carmen nodded and sighed as she sank down into the chair. "I think that is an excellent idea," she replied, slipping her shoes off and wiggling her toes before she grinned at the other two women. "My name is Carmen Walker-Reykill. As you can see, I'm pregnant. I'm having twins and all the joys that go with it, like swelling."

Jaguin paused when he heard his mate's swiftly inhaled breath when she heard Carmen's name. Just one more mystery among so many about her. He really did need to speak with Tandor. Jaguin was about to turn away, but the need to at least know her name ate at him. He drew in a deep breath.

"What are you called?" He asked suddenly, causing both women on the bed to jump. His mate frowned for a moment at him. Her lips tightened and she stared back at him with a wary expression. He knew she was debating whether to answer his question or not. "Please, I wish to know what you are called," he said in a softer tone.

"Sara. My name is Sara Wilson. This is Emma," she finally replied in a slightly uneven voice. Her hands trembled before she dropped them to the bed behind Emma so that he couldn't see them. "What is your name?"

A wave of pleasure coursed through him at her softly spoken question. "I am Jaguin," he replied with a slight bow. "I will leave you with Lady Carmen, Sara."

He saw her swallow and nod before he turned on his heel and left them alone. He knew that he needed to be careful how he approached Sara. She was like a wounded beast in the forest. If he was not careful, he could easily lose her either by fright or flight.

He turned the corner and stepped into Tandor's office. Tandor had activated the screen to give the women some privacy. Jaguin's gaze moved to the amber liquor that Tandor was pouring into a glass before the healer lifted it and held it out to him.

Stepping over to the chair opposite the desk, Jaguin sank down into it with a sigh. Sara, Sara Wilson. He now had a name to go with the face of his mate.

"Patience, Jaguin," Tandor quietly reminded him.

Jaguin lifted the drink in his hand and took a deep swig before he lowered the glass and gave the healer a sharp nod. Leaning his head back, he stared up at the ceiling for a moment before he returned his gaze to the healer. He stared at Tandor for a moment before he finally asked the question that was burning through him.

"What did the human male do to her, Tandor? I need to know what I am facing," he asked in a quiet voice.

* * *

Sara stared at the woman sitting in the chair with her feet propped up as if she was used to sitting in the medical unit on an alien ship. She watched as Carmen Walker-Reykill looked around the room with an appraising look. When the woman turned back to Sara and Emma, there was a gleam of amusement in her eyes.

"You know, my sister, Ariel, Trisha, and I tore the hell out of the medical unit on the *V'ager*," Carmen said with a grin before she grimaced and held up a swollen ankle. "I could still do it, but it wouldn't be as much fun now. The guys would scatter like mice before they'd take me on."

Sara frowned. "What do you mean – take you on? Did they beat you?" She asked in a hard tone.

Carmen threw her head back and laughed. The sound ended in a long sigh and she shook her head, sending her blonde hair dancing around it. Her brown eyes were lit with delight.

"No, they didn't beat me – more like I was the one doing the ass-kicking," she replied with another soft chuckle that finally sobered as she stared back at Emma and Sara. "I'm sorry," she finally said with a sad look.

Sara felt Emma tremble. At least, she thought it was Emma. It could have been her. The sorrow darkening the other woman's eyes was genuine. There was no longer any laughter or teasing.

"He wanted *you*," Sara finally murmured. "Why? What did you do that made him hate you so much?"

Carmen drew in a deep breath. Her eyes glittered for a moment with tears before she blinked and shook her head as if to regain control of her emotions. When she looked back at Sara, they held regret and a look of such deep sadness that it took Sara's breath away.

"You both deserve to know the truth," Carmen said in a quiet, somber tone. "Several years ago..."

Sara listened as Carmen explained that she and her human husband, Scott, had been hired to provide security for a political family in Colombia. Her heart ached for Carmen as she told Sara and Emma how Cuello had gunned them down while they were trying to protect the two children. Cuello had murdered Scott Walker in front of Carmen. Carmen had retaliated, stabbing Cuello in the upper thigh. One of Cuello's men had shot her, but she had survived. Unfortunately, the child she'd been carrying hadn't. Carmen's attack had cost Cuello his leg.

"He was insane," Carmen murmured with a shake of her head. "I had no idea he was kidnapping women who looked like me so he could take out his sick revenge. I searched for him for years. I had a lead on him when..."

"When... what?" Sara asked when Carmen paused and looked up at the ceiling.

Carmen looked back at Sara and gave her a crooked smile. "I woke up in a medical unit on an alien spaceship."

For the next two hours, Carmen told them about Abby Tanner and the attack on her that almost took

Carmen's life. Abby would have died if she hadn't discovered an alien spaceship and a wounded warrior on her mountain. The fight with Abby's kidnapper had left Carmen barely clinging to life until she was saved and given a new one.

"And now, Creon and I are expecting twins!" Carmen said, rubbing her rounded abdomen. Her grin widened when the door opened behind her.

Emma's soft gasp and quick push almost sent Sara tumbling backwards. Sara watched as Carmen's eyes once again glittered with amusement. Her entire face lit up with a flush and she winked at them.

"And so enters my mate," she chuckled, tilting her head back. "Hi Creon."

"Don't you 'Hi, Creon" me," the man growled. "I wake from my rest to discover you missing and in medical. I was worried until Cree told me that you were here just to visit with the women."

Carmen's lips drooped. "I thought I had given him the slip," she muttered with a sigh, rising stiffly out of the chair and giving a soft moan. A moment later, the moan turned to a gasp when she was swept off her feet. "Damn it, Creon, I'm pregnant, not sick!"

"She is fine, Lord Creon," Tandor said from behind them. "I have been monitoring her vitals. The girls are healthy as well."

Carmen's nose wrinkled and she shook her head. "I swear, I can barely go to the bathroom without you or Creon checking to make sure I'm okay," she grumbled.

Sara watched the display in amusement. Emma's soft giggle pulled a chuckle from her. A quick glance assured Sara that Emma was more relaxed than she was this morning. They watched as Creon carried Carmen out of the medical unit, closely followed by Tandor. Before the doors closed, the large golden creature that Sara had seen yesterday trotted into the room.

Three go out, one comes in. Make that two comes in, she thought when she saw the man – Jaguin – standing in the doorway.

Sara felt an unfamiliar rush of heat course through her. Her eyes narrowed when she saw Jaguin's lips briefly twitch, as if he knew she was aware of him, before they straightened. Returning her gaze to the golden creature, she started when she realized it had changed shape again. This time, it looked like an oversized puppy. She shook her head when it dropped another sloth on the bed.

"You know if you two keep bringing me these things, there won't be room for anything else in here," she replied dryly, arching one delicate brow.

The golden puppy looked at her for a moment before it turned to Emma and nudged the stuffed sloth onto her lap. It sat down, sneezed, and looked at Sara in triumph. Sara's gaze softened when Emma tenderly picked up the sloth and hugged it to her body.

"Thank you," Sara murmured, watching as Emma buried her face against the stuffed animal.

The puppy sneezed again and rested its head on the edge of the bed with a pleading look. Sara frowned in confusion. She wasn't sure what it wanted until a wave of warmth and an image of her stroking it flashed through her mind.

Shaking her head, she reached over and stroked the smooth, silky surface. She almost pulled away when several thin golden tentacles reached out. Her natural sense of curiosity developed over years of studying plants in the wild and doing research kept her hand still as they moved up her arm. She swallowed when the thin threads wrapped around her arm and formed an intricate bracelet.

"Dragons," she murmured, lifting her arm when it was finished.

"Yes," Jaguin replied quietly.

* * *

Jaguin stood still at the door. He had realized that both women tensed up whenever he got too close to them. Emma glanced nervously at him as she slid off the bed. He saw her cover her mouth with one hand to hide a yawn. A frown creased his brow when he saw how pale and tired she looked. Almost immediately, his gaze returned to Sara's face so he could search it for the same exhaustion.

"I think Emma wishes to lie down for a while," Sara finally said.

Jaguin nodded, not ready to leave yet. He had a little over an hour before he needed to report for duty. He took a step back before he stopped.

"Would you care to go for a walk? I could show you some of the ship if you'd like," he asked in a slightly awkward tone.

A faint flush darkened his cheeks. He felt like an adolescent seeing his first female! He tilted his head and returned Sara's surprised gaze.

"Emma...," Sara started to say, glancing at the other woman who had climbed back into her own bed and closed her eyes.

"My symbiot can stay with her," Jaguin responded with a hopeful look. "She seems adjusted to its presence and it will protect her."

Jaguin hid the wince when his symbiot sent a small shock through the cuffs on his arm in aggravation and turned its head to glare at him. He knew it wanted to be with Sara as well, but if this was the only way to convince her to go, it would have to stay. He gave Sara a weak smile when it shocked him again.

Will you knock it off! It isn't like you won't be there. You've got enough gold on her that I'm surprised she can even move, he silently growled back to it. *Besides, if this is going to work, I do have to be able to get near her as well!* He jumped when it sent another shock through him before it turned and padded over to where Emma was sleeping and laid down with a loud groan.

"Are you alright?" Sara asked, staring at him with a wary look.

Jaguin relaxed his expression and gave her a reassuring smile. "Yes, my symbiot and I were just having a slight disagreement," he admitted.

She looked at him with a doubtful expression before turning to glance at his symbiot. Her eyes widened when she saw it was shooting daggers at him. He didn't care. He wanted time with Sara, too! It was all over her. He could feel her warmth, the silkiness of her skin, her very heartbeat where the living metal rested against her flesh. It was driving him and his dragon crazy!

"You… are talking to that thing?" Sara asked in a hesitant voice, staring back and forth with a raised eyebrow. "How?"

Jaguin sent a heated glance at his symbiot before he returned his gaze to Sara. A mischievous smile lifted the corner of his mouth. Maybe he could use her curiosity to coax her to go for a walk with him.

"I will tell you… as we walk," he suggested, stepping to one side and raising his hand. "The *Horizon* isn't as large as the *V'ager*, but it is still a beautiful ship."

Sara studied him for several long moments before she slowly slid off the bed. She bit her lip, looking from his face to his outstretched palm, and then to the door before her gaze returned to his face again. He waited, staring deeply into her eyes. He knew the moment she made her decision. Once again, he was thankful she had such expressive eyes.

"Talking living metal, alien warships, and – dragons," she finally murmured, tilting her head to the side. "You have a lot of explaining to do."

Jaguin watched Sara's long curtain of hair fall to the side as she tilted her head to stare up at him with an uneasy look. She didn't trust him, but her curiosity was more powerful than her fear. His respect for her soared upward like his dragon enjoying the freedom of the skies.

The fingers of his right hand curled against his side. He hated the fear that remained like a ghostly shadow in her eyes. He slowly lowered his left hand and waited, suddenly unsure if she would come with him or not.

"No one will hurt you, Sara," Jaguin vowed in a soft voice. "I would kill anyone who tried."

He watched as she drew in a deep, unsteady breath. He saw her swallow and glance back at Emma. His symbiot lifted its head and returned her stare. Her shoulders drooped for a moment before she pulled her gaze back to him.

"Alien warship, huh?" She asked with an uneasy smile. "I've never been on one before."

"Then I am honored to guide you on your first voyage," Jaguin replied in a light tone, stepping to the side.

"This is all so strange," Sara whispered, fear gripping her again at the thought of stepping out of the room and into the unknown.

"It is strange in a good way," he responded, reaching up to tenderly run his fingers down along her cheek. His fingers froze a breath away from her skin when she stiffened. His lips pressed together for a brief second before he gently touched her cheek.

"It is just as I imagined," he murmured in a barely audible voice.

Sara remained frozen; her wary eyes wide as she stared back at him. Her lips parted and he could see the pulse on the side of her throat beating wildly. His gaze softened when he saw her fighting to hide her fear.

"What... What is as you imagined it?" She forced out in a husky tone.

"Your skin," he said, running his fingers down until he could cup her jaw in his hand. "Your skin is as soft as the petals of the lighted flowers that grow wild in the forest of my clan's mountains. So beautiful, like you."

* * *

Sara's mouth dropped open slightly when he dropped his hand to grasp hers. He lifted it to his mouth and pressed a kiss to the back of it. Her mind swirled in confusion, trying to comprehend that this alien male was actually flirting with her! She blinked in disbelief and stumbled when he gently tugged on her hand. She followed him in silence as he guided her out of the medical unit.

My skin is as soft as the lighted petals of the flowers that grow wild in the forest near his home? Maybe I did die and I'm in some type of alien parallel purgatory. She thought in disbelief as she walked beside him, trying to take in everything.

It suddenly dawned on her that this man, warrior, alien – whatever he was called – was spouting words that were similar to poetry. Sara shook her head again in shock. This was a first. None of her ex-boyfriends had ever said anything remotely poetic to her.

Chapter 5

Jaguin kept a tight grip on Sara's hand, afraid to release it in case she changed her mind. He could feel it tremble slightly. His mind raced to think of ways to soothe her fears. He grimaced when his mind went blank.

"What is the gold creature made of?" Sara asked, pushing her hair back with her free hand and breaking the tortured silence.

Jaguin flashed her a smile. "It is the blood of the Goddess," he replied.

Sara glanced at him with a raised eyebrow. "The blood of the Goddess?" She asked in a skeptical tone.

Jaguin shrugged. "That is what my people call it. Each warrior is given a small amount of her blood at birth. It grows alongside the warrior, living off the essences of our forms," he explained.

Sara shook her head and gently tugged on her hand. Jaguin didn't miss her quiet sigh of relief when he reluctantly released it or the fact that she put several steps between them. His fingers curled into a loose fist as he fought the urge to recapture her hand.

"It lives off the essences of your forms, as in plural? Are you saying your species can have more than one... form? And what do you mean by essence?" She asked in a tight, cautious tone.

Jaguin glanced at her with a wary expression. "My dragon and myself," he replied. "It feeds off of the essence that makes our forms possible."

He stopped several feet ahead of Sara when he realized that she was no longer walking beside him, but staring at him in wary disbelief. He moved from one foot to the other, stepping to one side when several warriors passed by. He didn't miss the way they looked at Sara, nor did he miss the way she shuddered and jerked to the side. Her eyes followed the warriors with dark distrust and more than a hint of fear.

"Dragons...," she whispered, still watching the other men until they disappeared around the corner at the end of the corridor. Only when they were no longer in sight did she turn back to him. "What... do you mean by you and your dragon?" She asked in a husky tone.

Jaguin's gaze softened. He could see the distress she was feeling reflected in her light brown eyes, though she was trying to hide it from him. He also saw a hint of curiosity.

"A Valdier warrior is made up of three parts: my two-legged form such as I am now, my dragon which I can shift into, and my symbiot which we both wear for protection," he replied, pointing to the band around his thick forearm. "It connects us as one."

* * *

Sara's eyes widened and her lips parted when she felt a wave of warmth spread out from the matching cuffs around her wrists and the necklace she was wearing. A shadowy image of a dragon appeared in her mind. It was silver with darker threads of green mixed in. Its golden eyes held a dark, red flame that seemed to dare her to look deeper.

Shocked, Sara shook her head to clear the vision. She blinked several times before the long corridor of the ship came back into view. A part of her felt like she was trapped in some type of alternate-reality show. Bowing her head, she drew in several deep, calming breaths. She focused her gaze on the tips of her boots.

"Focus," she whispered, staring at the dark brown tips. "You can do this. You've been through worse. You can do this."

She started when she felt a warm touch to her chin. Biting her lip, she tried to hide the fear threatening to send her into a panic attack. She reluctantly looked up and stared into Jaguin's warm, gold-colored eyes.

"You can do anything you want, Sara," he murmured, gently stroking her chin with the pad of his thumb.

"As long as it doesn't involve me returning home," she softy challenged, searching his gaze with her own.

"As long as it does not involve you returning to your world," he reluctantly agreed.

Sara's eyelashes lowered and she pulled her chin away. She didn't want to focus on the conflicting feelings his touch caused. She would do that when she was alone later. For right now, she decided the best thing to do was to allow her analytical side free rein. If she kept her attention on the science, she wouldn't have to deal with her emotional side or the overwhelming feeling of panic threatening to engulf her in its traitorous grip.

"What part of the ship are you going to show me besides the corridor?" She asked.

"There is only one section for now. I'm afraid I do not have much time before I must report for duty, but I thought I would show you a special place that you might enjoy visiting. It will give you a place other than the medical unit to explore," he explained with a wave of his hand.

Sara turned her head away from him when the sound of his husky voice swept over her, sending a shiver of warmth through her. She didn't understand what it was about him that made her respond this way. Her first thought was Stockholm Syndrome; where a captive felt an attraction to her captor.

That theory didn't work either, though. Jaguin wasn't exactly holding her prisoner. She knew if it hadn't been for him, Carmen, and the others, Sara and Emma would be dead now. It still didn't solve the problem that she was in a place not of her choosing.

I have to admit that I would rather be here than Cuello's compound any day, though, she silently conceded as she fell into step beside him.

* * *

Sara gently rubbed her forehead and tried to focus on where they were going. She listened as Jaguin quietly explained the different features of the ship as they walked by. It took her a few moments to realize that the soothing sound of his voice was helping the headache that had been a constant nuisance since she had woken up.

She didn't want to admit it, but the continual ache was beginning to worry her. She didn't know if it was a result of the beating and subsequent concussion, the stress of everything, or something the aliens may have inadvertently done, but *something* was wrong with her head.

Her mind felt fragmented, almost bruised. It was as if whatever had happened to her had opened a floodgate and now she couldn't shut down all the way so she could rest. Random thoughts sparked to life before burning out almost as quickly. She hadn't said anything to Tandor, but if it continued, she would.

Yet with Jaguin's voice flowing over her, the throbbing faded to a dull, persistent ache. The pain still made it difficult to concentrate on every word the huge man next to her was saying, but at least the full drum corps that had been playing in her temple had decreased to a low thump for the moment.

A tired sigh escaped her and she dropped her hand. She could feel the thin, gold creature moving on her. It was as if it could sense her distress. A shiver ran through her and goosebumps appeared on her arms. She didn't want to admit that it was freaking her out – but, it was freaking her out.

"Is it possible to have this stuff go back to you?" she asked in a husky voice before she cleared her throat.

"Stuff?" Jaguin asked in confusion, glancing down at Sara's pale face. "Are you unwell? You appear to be paler than before. I should have considered that it was too soon for you to leave the medical unit."

"No, it's not that. I'm fine. It's just, I'm not used to wearing jewelry, especially jewelry that is alive. The way it is moving around on me is freaking me out just a little. I don't... I need it off of me," she ended, coming to a stop again in the corridor as she tried to push down the panic that was rising inside her. "Please."

She saw his expression twist in confusion and disappointment before he nodded. Almost immediately, the gold on her arms and around her neck dissolved. She watched in fascination as the gold reformed into the tiny shape of a dragon.

"Oh!" She whispered, startled as it floated in front of her. Unable to resist, she lifted her hand to hover just under it. She glanced over to Jaguin with wide eyes. "Can I...?"

"Yes, you may touch it all you wish. You cannot harm it – and it would never harm you, Sara. My symbiot wishes only to protect you," Jaguin murmured, turning so that he stood in front of her.

She watched as he lifted one hand and extended a finger. The delicate dragon landed on his outstretched digit, balancing as it folded its nearly transparent wings back against its body. A small, bemused smile curved Sara's lips when the golden creature tilted its head at her and nodded as if agreeing with Jaguin.

Sara took a step closer, mesmerized by the beauty of the alien form. She jumped when it reached up and gripped her finger when she went to stroke it. She glanced up at Jaguin in uncertainty.

"It will not harm you," he assured her again.

Sara bit her lip and gave him a trembling smile before her gaze moved back to the creature she was holding. It now had both its front and back feet wrapped around her finger. The creature was so long that its tail wound down and around not just her hand, but her wrist as well. A soft, startled giggle escaped Sara when the golden head bent and the dragon suddenly rubbed its cheek against the tip of her finger.

"This is amazing," she breathed out in a tone filled with awe. It seemed different now that she wasn't wearing it. She glanced quickly up at Jaguin before she returned her gaze to the symbiot. "I know you said it was made from the blood of the Goddess, but that doesn't make much sense to me. Do you know what the composition of the matter is?" She asked, gently stroking it.

Jaguin shrugged. "No. It has been with me since shortly after my birth; we simply accept it for what it is, a living metal," he replied with a grin. "One day soon, I will show you. For now, let me show you where the warriors go when they wish to relax. There are three such rooms on board. They are necessary during long voyages."

Sara absently nodded, too focused on the small dragon wrapped around her hand to pay attention to the fact that they were standing in front of a set of double doors. She briefly glanced up when it opened, then looked back at her hand. It took a moment for her brain to connect with what her eyes had seen in that brief glance. Her head jerked up again, making her wince at the sudden movement when it caused another brief wave of pain to sweep through her head.

If her jaw had dropped at the sight of the dragon she was holding, it was nothing compared to what it did at the sight in front of her now. Without realizing it, she cradled the dragon protectively against her chest as she took a step into the room. She stopped ten feet inside and turned in a tight circle. All around her were plants – beautiful alien plants in all different shapes, colors, and sizes.

Her head tilted back as her gaze ran up an enormous tree. It rose up to where the ceiling was supposed to be. A wave of dizziness swept through her when she saw brilliant blue skies and white, fluffy clouds instead. She wasn't even aware that her knees had given out until she felt a pair of strong, warm arms wrap around her.

Her head rolled against his shoulder as he tenderly lifted her into his arms. A wave of panic started to rise, but it quickly settled when he stepped along a path and gently set her down on a lounge.

"What is this place?" She asked in a husky tone, still holding the symbiot close to her chest.

Jaguin sat down beside her and tenderly brushed a strand of her hair from her pale face. She ignored the frown creasing his brow when he felt her wince at the touch. Instead, she leaned back, amazed at the warmth that immediately surrounded her.

"This is where our symbiots come to play and where we come to relax. It is a combination of real plants, our symbiots playing, and hologram technology. In here, we can create just about anything or any place that we wish. Sometimes, groups of warriors come here to perfect their skills in hunting or tracking. At other times, we come here to be close to our home world. Space, and the life of a warrior, can be a very lonely existence, even with our symbiot and dragon for company...," he explained, his voice fading on the last words. He turned to gaze down at her. "I hoped you would enjoy this."

Sara's gaze turned back to him and she frowned in confusion. "You keep saying your dragon. Do you mean like this?" She asked, holding up the symbiot still wrapped around her hand.

Jaguin shook his head and looked around the forest he had programmed into the computer. Sara closely observed the flicker of expressions that crossed his face. He appeared deep in thought, as if he was arguing with himself. After several long seconds, he released an exasperated breath and turned to give her a crooked smile.

"My dragon says you need to see him to understand," Jaguin finally admitted. "I am afraid it will scare you to see me shift so soon."

Sara couldn't quite hide the amused grin that was pulling at the corner of her mouth. Once again, she felt like she was in that alternate world, much like Alice must have felt when she fell down the rabbit's hole. She looked thoughtfully down at the symbiot she was holding. It was staring back at her, its small body shimmering with the colors of the room. A familiar wave of warmth swept through her hand, spreading upward. The image of the silver dragon once again flickered through her mind.

"I think...." She paused and drew in a deep breath before she looked at him again. "I think I would like to see your dragon."

Jaguin's hand rose to touch her cheek. Sara instinctively flinched before she could stop herself. His hand wavered just a breath away from her skin before he nodded and let it fall back to the lounge. She sat up when he rose and took several steps away from her.

"Do not be afraid," Jaguin cautioned her. "My dragon would never harm you."

Sara nodded, unable to speak. She lifted her left hand and pressed her trembling fingers to her lips. Her eyes widened when Jaguin's body shimmered for a brief second. In the blink of an eye, the man was gone and in his place stood a....

"Oh, my! You really can shift into a dragon!" Sara whispered in shock.

She lowered her hand back to her lap and just stared in wonder. It was too unbelievable to be afraid. He was just... beautiful! The golden symbiot dragon in her hand launched itself into the air and flew to the large dragon. A trembling laugh escaped her when the silver dragon puffed out a series of small smoke rings. The symbiot twisted and turned, going through the center of each one before landing on top of the dragon's head.

Sara rose to her feet. She swayed as the world tilted for a moment and her trembling legs threatened to give out again. A soft gasp escaped her when she was suddenly steadied. Her hands dropped down instinctively to grip the tail that was wrapped around her waist, holding her up.

"You... They are soft and smooth," she murmured, stroking her fingertips over the scales. "So, beautiful."

Sara stared down in fascination, mesmerized by the delicate texture and unusual markings on the scales. They were varying shades of silver that appeared to shimmer and change, but that wasn't the only thing that held her in awe. Each scale had an intricate design. There was a thread of dark green running around the edge of each one.

She bent closer and traced it with her finger, watching the colors inside the thin vein swirl. A low, gruff purr startled her, and she glanced up, almost bumping her head on the dragon's chin as he watched what she was doing. Her lips parted and her eyes locked with the golden gaze staring back at her.

"You are... the most unusual creature I have ever seen in my life," she confessed, hesitantly reaching up to touch his snout. "The scientist in me wants to know all about you, while the woman in me..." Her voice faded and she shook her head and closed her eyes.

"The woman in you what?" Jaguin asked in a husky voice.

Sara's eyes popped open at the sound of his voice. Gone was the tail that was holding her. Now, a pair of strong arms were wrapped around her waist. Sara started to answer when the nagging pain in her head suddenly exploded and a soft moan escaped her instead.

"Sara.... Sara, what is it?"

Jaguin's voice seemed to be coming from a long way away. Sara tried to focus, but the pain in her head was increasing to the point that she was afraid she was going to be sick. She was vaguely aware of being lifted.

"Tandor, this is Jaguin. I am bringing Sara back to medical. Something is wrong. She is in pain. We are currently on Deck Four in Rec Two."

Jaguin was speaking in a soft, urgent voice. Sara wanted to explain that it was her head, but all she could do was keep her eyes closed and pray for relief from the agonizing pain threatening to split her brain in half.

Sara moaned again as another shaft of pain pierced her. A shudder went through her when she felt the warm liquid of the symbiot dissolve and it began to move over her skin. She lifted her hand in a vain attempt to push it away, but it was too difficult to fight it.

"What happened to her?"

Sara heard Carmen's familiar voice ask. A soft whimper escaped her when the pain increased. She tried to turn her head into Jaguin's chest when she felt a slender hand against her brow.

"I do not know; she suddenly collapsed. I need to get her to medical. My symbiot is trying to discover what has happened to her," Jaguin's said impatiently.

"What is her name?" Another voice asked.

This time it was the voice of a woman that Sara didn't recognize. She had not known there were other women besides herself, Emma, and Carmen on board. The voice held the same tone of authority that Tandor's did when he was talking to others that came into the medical unit.

"Sara," Jaguin replied in a harsh tone edged with worry.

"Audrey is a human doctor," Carmen was explaining.

"Sara, can you tell me where you are hurting?" Audrey asked in a calm voice, keeping pace with them from the sound of her voice near Sara's head.

Sara struggled to push the pain away. She'd done it before back at the compound, but this was different. This was striking her from the inside out, instead of the other way around.

"Head," Sara was finally able to whisper.

She winced when a cold hand pressed to her brow. In the background, all she could hear was the soft sound of the lift as it moved and the breathing of those in the enclosed area. Another whimper escaped her when the woman gently lifted her left eyelid.

"Her left pupil is slightly dilated. Do either of you know if Sara was in an accident or if she received any type of head injury?" Audrey asked.

"Yes," Carmen replied.

"Do you know what is wrong with her?" Jaguin demanded as the lift began to slow.

Sara tried to follow the conversation, but the pain was too much. When she felt the inky blackness of unconsciousness reaching for her, she let go. She was so tired of being in pain. For a brief moment, a wave of regret swept through her that she wouldn't be there for Emma, or get a chance to explore the wonderful room Jaguin had shown her.

Or his dragon, she vaguely thought as she slipped into the black hole sucking her downward away from the pain.

Chapter 6

Jaguin paused outside the medical unit and drew in a deep breath. Even after three days, he was still fighting the urge to kill Tandor. He kept reminding himself that: one, it would just upset Sara and Emma; and two, Creon would not take kindly to him killing the only healer on board that Carmen trusted.

Creon was not amused when Jaguin told him that the human healer could take over. He knew he was being unreasonable, but from what he had deduced from the conversation between Audrey and Tandor, Sara had come very close to dying – again. If his symbiot hadn't found and repaired the small blood vessel that had begun to leak on the left side of Sara's brain, she would have died.

Jaguin flexed his fingers and rolled his shoulders before he stepped up to the door. It slid silently open and his gaze immediately narrowed in on the room where Sara and Emma had been staying. A flash of panic swept through him when he saw it was empty. Stepping into the room, he paused near the entrance. Both beds were neatly made and all the stuffed creatures his symbiot and he had given to Sara were gone.

He quickly turned his head around when he heard a sound to his left. The scowl on his face deepened when he saw Tandor staring back at him with a wary gaze. He turned to the healer and folded his arms across his chest.

"Where is she?" Jaguin demanded in a blunt tone.

Tandor shook his head. "I released them," he said, raising his hands up when Jaguin dropped his arms and took a menacing step toward him. "I did a complete scan on both women and reviewed the results with Gunner's... mate," Tandor added quickly. "She is a remarkable healer."

Jaguin frowned when he heard the slight edge to Tandor's voice. His first thought was to check for himself that Sara was alright. It took him a moment to remember that he was not wearing any of his symbiot. In his panic, he had ordered all of it to stay with her. It hadn't taken much convincing. His symbiot had readily complied. It was Jaguin and his dragon who were having a difficult time with the withdrawal.

"You are sure she is well? She came very close to dying just days ago. Shouldn't she stay a few more days, just to make sure this does not happen again?" Jaguin demanded with a frown of worry.

Tandor's lips twitched. Jaguin once again curled his fingers in an effort not to wrap them around Tandor's neck. It wasn't funny. He knew he was being overprotective, but he had a reason to be. Sara had come close to dying not once, but twice. Not only that, he was discovering it wasn't easy having a true mate, especially when she was clueless of that fact.

"Would you care for a drink?" Tandor asked, stepping back and waving his hand toward his office. "I assume you are off duty."

Jaguin wavered, turning his gaze toward the empty beds, then to the door before he released a tired grunt. He'd known it was too early for Sara to be awake, but he had needed to see her. His plan had been to slip in and reassure himself that she was fine before returning to his own cabin to rest for a few hours.

"Yes, I am off duty," Jaguin replied, lifting a hand and running it through his hair. "I would like a drink."

"I thought you looked like you could use one," Tandor chuckled and shook his head. "It is not easy finding your true mate. I have a whole new appreciation for that fact now."

Jaguin frowned and studied Tandor's wistful expression. "You have found your true mate?" He asked in surprise.

"Yes," Tandor responded with a sigh. "But, therein lies another problem. Come, I am off duty unless someone gets injured enough to require more than their symbiot's assistance. I can only hope that they don't. It has actually been rather boring since Carmen is no longer allowed to challenge them."

Jaguin chuckled and nodded. "I enjoyed watching her with Cree and Calo. She still tries to test their abilities, and their patience."

"Not as much as their mate does," Tandor retorted with a dry laugh.

"So I've heard. I am glad that they have found their mate. I have always respected the powers of the Twin Dragons. I, for one, would not have wanted to fight them if it had become necessary," Jaguin chuckled again and sat down in the seat across from Tandor's desk.

He reached over and picked up the drink that Tandor poured for him and placed it on the edge of the desk. They sat in silence for several minutes, each lost in their own thoughts. Jaguin stared moodily down into his drink.

"Does she know?" Tandor asked quietly, breaking the silence.

Jaguin glanced up with a frown. "Does she know what?" He asked in a cautious tone.

Tandor released a sigh and sat back in his chair. "Does Sara know that she is your true mate?" He asked patiently. "Did you tell her? Does she know what it means? She said you showed her your dragon. She was curious if all of us were capable of shifting. She appears to accept that you are a regular visitor. I am curious as to how she reacted to your claim."

Jaguin thought about Tandor's questions. In all honesty, he had assumed that Sara recognized his claim. A female in his world recognized immediately that if a male, along with his symbiot and dragon, accepted her, she was his true mate. It had never occurred to him that Sara might not know what they were to each other, what it meant. A soft groan escaped Jaguin at the thought and he reached up to run a tired hand down his face.

"I don't know," he finally confessed, shaking his head and looking at Tandor with a slight scowl. "My father and the other men in the village did not do a very good job of explaining all of this, you know."

Tandor released a dry chuckle. "You can't blame them, this is new to all of us. I've talked a bit with Carmen. She said there is a thing called love at first sight. That did not make sense to me until I also asked Audrey. She explained that there is a chemical humans release, which causes a reaction between the male and female. This chemical helps boost their attraction to each other. She also stated that it is not something that will seal the bond between them the way it does for us, nor is it always necessary for the chemical to be present for two of her species to have a relationship. This is much more complex than with our species. All we have to do is wait for our symbiot and dragon to agree with us to know that we have found our true mate," he explained with a tight smile that did not quite reach his eyes.

"Yes, but what if the female does not agree?" Jaguin asked before he lifted his glass to his lips and swallowed the remaining contents. Placing the glass on the desk, he rose to his feet. "Where is Sara's living quarters?" He asked.

Tandor rose to his feet and stretched. "Sara and Emma are on Deck Two. Carmen thought it would be nice to have them close to Creon's and her quarters," he replied with a tired sigh of his own.

Jaguin nodded and started to turn before he paused. Glancing at Tandor, he opened his mouth to say something, but he closed it again and just nodded. He wasn't the type to share his emotions, even with the healer.

He quietly exited the medical unit and headed down to Deck Two. A short time later, he stepped off the lift and strode down the corridor. He was surprised when he saw his symbiot trotting down the passageway toward him before it turned and disappeared into a small lounge set aside for those seeking a place to sit and relax. Each deck of the ship had many of them. It was necessary for longer voyages.

Striding forward, he paused in the open doorway. Sara was standing at the wide window looking out at the darkness beyond, her arms wrapped protectively around her waist. He watched in silence as his symbiot lifted its head toward her and nudged her right elbow. She lifted a hand to wipe at her cheek before lowering it to rest on his symbiot's head. At that moment, Jaguin wanted more than anything to know what she was feeling.

He lifted a hand toward his symbiot and several small threads shot out toward him. He waited as they wrapped around his wrists. Almost immediately, he could feel the blinding grief, anger, and despair.

"Sara," Jaguin murmured in a quiet voice.

She stiffened and hastily wiped at her face again before turning. The haunted look was back in her eyes. He also noticed the dark circles under them. She was not sleeping.

"Jaguin! I thought you were working," she exclaimed, forcing a smile to her lips.

"I am off now," he replied, stepping into the room. "I stopped by the medical unit to see you. Tandor told me that you and Emma were moved to your own quarters. You are well?"

He watched as she swallowed and half turned back to the window so he couldn't see her eyes. Her lips parted and he knew that she was going to tell him that she was fine, she always did, but he could see the truth in her eyes.

"I'm… okay," she finally whispered, looking back out the window.

"Please talk to me," Jaguin said, stepping closer to her.

For several long seconds, she didn't respond. He could see her drawing in deep breaths. In the reflection of the window, he could see the desolation in her eyes. He took another step closer. Lifting his hands, he carefully rested them on her hips. A shudder ran through her body and she stiffened before relaxing back against him and bowed her head.

"Every time I close my eyes, I see him," she whispered in a husky voice. "I can't seem to turn my brain off anymore. Audrey said that it isn't unusual for someone who has gone through a traumatic event. She is trying to help me, but I think it is getting worse. I'm so tired."

Jaguin could feel her fatigue. His mind raced, trying to find a way to help her. He didn't know why he thought of an incident that had happened in his youth, but it seemed right to share it.

He carefully turned Sara and guided her over to the long couch that faced the windows. He motioned for her to sit. She moved silently, as if unable to resist his guidance. He sank down next to her and turned her so that she was resting against his body. His arms slid around her waist and he rested his cheek against her hair. With a quick thought, a portion of his symbiot dissolved and covered them with a thin blanket of gold while another small part made a pillow for his head.

"I don't think I'll ever get used to this," she murmured. "It's cool – and weird at the same time."

A soft chuckle escaped Jaguin as Sara relaxed against him. He leaned his head back and gazed out the window. He could feel his own fatigue pulling at him.

"My home is in the eastern mountains of Valdier. It is a beautiful place. The trees grow upward, straining to touch the sky. At times, a thick fog rolls down the slopes, making it almost magical. There are over thirty waterfalls, some high in the mountains and others near the valley floor where my village is located."

"It sounds beautiful," Sara murmured, snuggling closer when he wrapped his arms around her. "How do you know there are thirty of them?"

Jaguin released a sigh of contentment. "When I was a youngling, I was determined to find every one of them, including the Hidden Falls," he explained in a soft voice.

"Hidden falls?" Sara asked.

Jaguin smiled, he could hear the curiosity in her voice now. She had settled closer to him, no longer holding herself slightly away. Deep down, he felt his dragon's sigh of contentment.

"Deep in the mountains there is said to be a magical valley. At the end is a great cavern where the Hidden Falls lie deep inside. Crystal deposits have collected over the centuries and at sunrise and sunset each day the light from the sun streams through an opening in the rocks causing the crystals to refract the light. It turns the falls a multitude of colors," Jaguin said before yawning.

"Did you see it? The light changing the falls to a different color?" Sara asked in a hushed tone.

"Yes, many times," Jaguin murmured. "You would love the valley. There are many unique plants and animals that live there."

Jaguin's voice faded as the exhaustion from so many sleepless nights finally caught up with him. The warmth of Sara's body pressed against his and the calming of his dragon at last sent a wave of contentment through him. A smile curved his lips and he fell into a light sleep.

"Jaguin?" Sara whispered, twisting her head when he didn't answer her. She stared at his relaxed face for several long seconds before a confused frown creased her brow.

"Why do I feel safe with you when I don't know what it means to be safe anymore?" She murmured.

"Because you are my true mate," he responded in a barely audible voice.

Sara laid her head back against Jaguin. She started to stiffen when she felt his hands move across her stomach, but he only threaded his fingers together before relaxing even more. She could tell from the soft snores that he was really asleep.

Turning her head, she stared out the window in confusion. How on Earth had she ended up in his arms like this? Better yet, what in the hell did he mean by 'you are my true mate'? She'd heard Carmen refer to Creon as such. Did that mean that Jaguin thought of her as...

"Holy shit!" Sara whispered, her eyes growing wide when she felt the warmth of the symbiot's touch within her again and the faint purr of the silver dragon in her head.

Her gaze lowered to where she was absently stroking the golden blanket covering them. She was intelligent enough to put two and two together and come up with four. A slight, disbelieving snort escaped her. It really was four if she thought about Jaguin, his dragon, his symbiot, and herself all together.

"Shit! I've not only fallen down the rabbit's hole, I've ended up in Narnia," she groaned, closing her eyes and shaking her head. "All I need now is a group of enraged dwarves looking for their palace of gold."

The sudden image of the silver dragon actually rolling its eyes at her comment had her biting her lip to keep from laughing. Another wave of warmth swept through her. She opened her eyes and stared out at the dark space.

"This is still better than Cuello's compound," she whispered to herself. "It is strange beyond imagination, but… beautiful. I just wish I knew how it was going to end. I don't know what to do."

Sara started to move when she felt the strange sensation against her skin. She released an exasperated sigh when she recognized it as the symbiot. Shortly after she woke up in the medical unit, she had discovered she was once again draped in the living jewelry. No matter how much she had argued with the creature, it had refused to dissolve again.

Sara softly groaned. If anything, she was wearing even more of the delicate pieces. When she had snapped at it impatiently, the symbiot had given her such a woeful look of hurt and distress that she had finally given up.

"You really don't fight fair, you know that, don't you?" Sara demanded in a soft voice. "None of you do. Something tells me that my life is going to become even more complicated very soon."

A barely audible giggle of amusement escaped Sara when Jaguin's hands tightened around her as if in agreement. She realized she was well and truly stuck for the time being. She felt her exhaustion pull at her.

Maybe, just maybe, Jaguin and his strange assortment of alternate personalities can keep the nightmares at bay, she thought as she fell into a deep, restful sleep.

Chapter 7

Several days later, Sara woke with a start. She looked frantically around the room, trying to get her bearings. She was in the cabin they had given her a few days earlier. It was connected with Emma's cabin next door. Her gaze swung around and connected with Emma's worried blue eyes. Sara gave the woman sitting on the edge of her bed a rueful smile and relaxed back against the pillows.

"I was yelling again, wasn't I?" Sara murmured.

"Yes," Emma replied in a barely audible voice before she gave a haunted smile. "You were cursing, too."

Sara shook her head and pushed herself up into a sitting position. Emma had finally begun to talk again, but only to her. It wasn't much, but it was a little.

"I was dreaming that I was back at the compound again," Sara admitted, glancing at Emma before she drew her knees up and wrapped her arms around them. "I thought I was getting better."

"You are, when you are with... him," Emma forced out.

Sara glanced up again. A sardonic smile twisted her lips. She knew who 'him' was – Jaguin. It seemed like the only time she really fell into a deep sleep was when she was with him, or at least it appeared that way from the last two nights she had woken from a nightmare. On those nights, she had escaped to the lounge Jaguin had found her in before so she wouldn't disturb Emma who liked to leave the door between their rooms open, only to find Jaguin there waiting for her.

Three times now, the first night and the last two, he had wrapped his arms around her and held her close while he told her a little more about the beautiful Hidden Falls, the vast mountain meadows, and the bountiful plants and animals that lived in the mist-covered mountains before he fell asleep.

"Argh, I hate this," Sara moaned, dropping her head against her knees.

Sara's eyes burned with tears as she felt Emma's soft touch run over her hair. She hated – absolutely hated – feeling out of control. With an annoyed sniff, she rubbed her nose against the covers and lifted her head. Her jaw tightened in determination. She wasn't going to become dependent on anyone. It was time she started taking control of her emotions, instead of the other way around.

"There is a room on the fourth deck that Jaguin took me to," Sara said, staring back at Emma. "It has all kinds of plants in it. I want to start learning more about them. Do you want to come with me?"

Emma quickly shook her head and scooted off the edge of the bed. Sara watched as her friend glanced around the room in panic. Throwing the covers back, Sara slid out of the bed and walked over to where Emma was standing with her arms wrapped around her waist and her head bowed.

"They aren't going to hurt us, Emma. I just know it. Just look at Audrey and Carmen. They have the men on this ship wrapped around their fingers. The guys – they aren't like Cuello and his men," Sara said.

"I... know," Emma replied, looking up at Sara, her eyes shimmering with unshed tears. "I just... want to... go... home. My mom...."

Sara heard Emma's voice fade and watched as the young girl looked toward the long, narrow window outside of the bedroom. Reaching out, Sara wrapped her arms around Emma and pulled her close as they offered strength and solidarity to one another.

"Perhaps one day," Sara murmured.

She released Emma when the other woman nodded and pulled back. Emma reached up, pushed her hair away from her face with a shaky hand, and gave Sara a rueful smile. The haunting sadness in Emma's eyes caused Sara to realize, deep down, that she was losing her.

"I have to fight. We have to fight. We can't give up, Emma. We didn't when Cuello held us prisoner and we won't now. This is different, we may be far away from home, but that doesn't mean we'll never see it again. Carmen left it and came back once, so can we."

Emma stared back at her for a moment before she nodded in agreement. For the first time, Sara saw a glimmer of hope reflected in Emma's eyes. It was small, but it was there.

"I'm... glad... you are here, Sara," Emma said.

"Me, too," Sara responded with a sigh. "Try to get some rest. I'm going to find that room Jaguin showed me. I've never liked being cooped up."

Emma nodded again before she turned and silently walked to her bedroom. Sara quickly changed into the jeans, shirt, and boots that were given to them. She picked up the dark brown leather jacket, and pulled it on. Twisting her hair into a messy bun, she glanced around for a way to hold it in place. A startled squeak escaped her when a ribbon of gold dissolved and turned into a large hair clip.

"Just like I was thinking," she muttered with a shake of her head as she reached out for it. "You might come in handy after all."

She turned when a movement by the door caught her attention. The larger form of the symbiot was sitting in the doorway. Resting her hands on her hips, Sara scowled down at the oversized golden sloth.

"Too slow. I think a jaguar would be better," Sara stated with a raised eyebrow.

Within seconds, the sleek form of the cat found in the jungles of South America stood in front of her. Sara released a soft whistle. She really needed to do some closer observations on the symbiot. It had pulled the image from her mind and transformed almost simultaneously.

"I really have a lot to learn about this new world," she muttered, stepping through the doorway.

* * *

Jaguin's dragon stretched before releasing a shudder of contentment. He could feel his dragon's pleasure and excitement at being free for a while. He wouldn't have much time before he headed down to the room where he hoped to see Sara. It was the only time he had with her each day and he cherished each moment.

Enjoy your time, my friend, Jaguin encouraged.

Mate like me, his dragon grumbled.

She has only seen you once. Creon cautioned that the humans are not used to dragons. We need to give her time to accept us, Jaguin insisted.

She accept me, his dragon replied with a snort. *She touch me.*

Yes, when she was ill, Jaguin retorted. *She might not remember much.*

You just jealous. She like me better, his dragon snorted.

She does not! Jaguin snapped hotly. *She falls asleep in my arms.*

His dragon released a rumbling laugh. *You one who falls asleep,* his dragon chortled.

I... Jaguin's growl faded when the door to the room opened.

She here! Mate come!

Jaguin would have shifted if his dragon hadn't overpowered his demand. He was so shocked by his dragon's refusal to bow to his will that he was speechless for a moment. Never before had his dragon absolutely refused to listen to him. Curious, he decided to see what his dragon would do – and how Sara would respond.

She like me better than you, his dragon insisted, climbing down from the perch it had climbed up onto.

She does not, Jaguin mumbled in a grouchy tone. *If you scare her, I'm not letting you back out.*

Humph! His dragon responded with another snort.

Both of them watched in silence as Sara entered the room. She looked around for several minutes before a delighted smile curved her lips. It was the first natural smile that Jaguin had seen in her eyes.

She beautiful, his dragon breathed, staring in delight at his mate.

Yes, she is, Jaguin silently agreed.

* * *

"This is fantastic," Sara murmured, stepping along the path.

She stretched her hand out to lightly touch a thick leaf. It looked like it had a slightly fuzzy texture. Her fingers passed through the leaf, drawing a startled hiss from her. It was just an image.

Bending down on one knee, she examined the plant closer. The underside was smooth and shiny. The veins running through the leaf pulsed with a light yellow luminescence. It was incredible to believe that the leaf was just a three-dimensional image.

"It looks so real," she murmured to herself, reaching up to touch it again.

Sara shook her head before rising to her feet again. She glanced over the large area, wondering just how large it really was. It was slightly different from the last time she was here.

She giggled as she ran her hand through the plants. Some glowed brighter while others folded into themselves. She wondered if they did that in real life. Something told her that they did. Deep down, she could feel the excitement of the new discovery course through her, revitalizing her. This is what she loved. This is where she belonged – among the plants.

Sara walked slowly down the path that appeared almost like magic before her. Jaguin's symbiot padded beside her, gazing around in curiosity. She instinctively lowered her hand and rubbed its head when it lifted it toward her.

"You know, I think you need a name. I've never heard Jaguin call you anything but 'my symbiot'. Do you have a name?"

The golden head shook back and forth violently before the creature sneezed. A soft laugh escaped Sara and she took the movement to mean that the symbiot did not have a name. She stopped and tilted her head, gazing thoughtfully down at it. She folded an arm around her stomach and balanced the elbow of her other arm on it as she tapped her chin.

"Mm, let's see. You're gold and you can change. You remind me a little of the Little Honey Oakleaf Hydrangea, also known as the Hydrangea Quercifolia. That is a bit of a mouthful, so how about Honey? I'm not sure if you are a male or a female or both, but I like the sound of it, what about you?" Sara asked after several moments.

The sleek jaguar shivered with delight, sending a ripple of colors over its body. Sara laughed when it raised one paw and licked it. She swore that it looked like it was licking honey off of its paw.

"You even look like honey when you do that," she chuckled. "So, Honey, are these plants like the ones on your world?"

The jaguar tilted its head and gazed back at her. Sara drew in a startled breath when vivid images filled her mind. For several breathtaking moments she was lost in another world – Jaguin's world. She could see the mountains that he'd told her about and the numerous waterfalls.

She closed her eyes and focused. Her body swayed as she found herself soaring upward over the tall trees, then back down to skim along the tops of the sea of purple grass.

In the distance, a path opened up into the forest. A second later, she swept through the entrance between the thick trunks and into the shadows. Her lips parted when she felt herself land along the trail similar to what she was walking on.

Colorful veins with vivid flowers, some the size of a large dinner plate, glowed in the dark recesses of the trees. Her hand reached for one of the plants. Disappointment swept through her when all she felt was empty air.

Sara opened her eyes and blinked rapidly to bring the room back into focus. Her mouth snapped shut and she took half a step back in surprise when she found herself staring at her own reflection in a pair of glittering gold eyes.

"Jaguin!" She breathed before drawing in another breath. Her gaze turned from surprise to confusion. "At least, I think it is you, unless you call your dragon something else."

Her eyebrow rose when the large silver dragon in front of her suddenly sat down and sneezed. An amused smile curved her lips when the dragon opened its mouth and gave her a toothy grin. Sara slowly walked forward, curious to see if what she remembered was real. Lifting her hand, she carefully ran her fingers over one nostril when he lowered its head to her.

"Just as soft as I remember," she murmured. "I wasn't expecting you here. I guess the other room would have been a bit crowded for this form, huh?"

The dragon rubbed its cheek against her outstretched palm. Sara took that as agreement. Stepping closer, she studied the dragon. It was even more beautiful than she remembered. It looked much like the ancient dragons from mythology. She vaguely wondered if perhaps at some time in history one of the Valdier spaceships had landed on Earth and they were spotted by humans in their dragon form. It would explain where some of the drawings and paintings had come from.

"So beautiful," Sara murmured, running her hand over the long snout and over a ridged eyebrow. "Do you mind if I touch you? I'd like to look at you more closely – if it won't offend you."

Sara's breath caught in her throat when the dragon bent its head and nudged her. Taking that as a yes, she returned her attention to where her hand lay. She swallowed as she ran her fingers up along one ear. It twitched and a low rumbling purr escaped the dragon as if it was trying to smother a laugh.

"Are you ticklish?" Sara asked with a curious smile.

She scratched the dragon behind the ear and a low moan filled the air. Scratching a little harder, she bit her lip when his back left foot began to thump against the floor. Leaning forward, she couldn't resist whispering in his ear.

"I used to have an old hound dog that did the same thing when I scratched him there," she shared before pulling back. "He was my best friend when I was ten. I grew up in the lower mountain region of the Appalachian Mountains. My mom had me when she was young, though that really shouldn't have made much difference. She dumped me on my aunt who was already raising her own kids and a bunch of others. I was the only girl. My aunt said she'd had enough of taking care of her sisters to know that she didn't want any more girls in the house." Sara paused for a moment; her hand rested on the side of the dragon's neck and her fingers absently traced the scales as she thought back to her youth. "It wasn't the best way to be raised, but it could have been worse," she continued in a soft voice. "I learned to fight and I

learned what I didn't want my life to be like. But...."
A small smile curved her lips and she turned to look
into the golden eyes watching her with a fierce
intensity that made her self-conscious. She released a
derisive laugh and shook her head. "I also discovered
what I did want. I loved running through the
mountains and exploring the different plants that
grew there. I became more fascinated about the plants
when I learned that they could help heal. I cut my
foot and it quickly became infected. My aunt was not
the best mother, but she knew the medicinal
properties of the plants. I watched and learned. Then,
when I was fifteen, one of my teachers opened my
eyes to the power of a good education. I left home at
sixteen and never looked back. My aunt didn't think
an education was necessary for living on the
mountain. I was expected to marry a miner and have
a bunch of kids. I wanted more than that. I wanted to
explore the world, and I wanted to find a cure to help
prevent common diseases and infections from turning
fatal. My best friend died from the flu."

She fell silent, lost in her memories. She thought of
her best friend from kindergarten through fifth grade.
Delilah Rosewater had been shy, but had a heart of
gold. She hadn't made fun of Sara for wearing her
cousins' hand-me-downs. When the other kids had
called her Tom for wearing boy's clothing, Delilah
had scolded them. She'd shared her lunch with Sara
when one of her cousins stole her sandwich.

Delilah had been the daughter of the local
librarian and a coal miner. She'd helped Sara learn to

read and had brought her books from the library. She had even invited Sara to her birthday parties.

Towards the end of their fifth grade year, a deadly flu virus swept through the mountains. Sara had a minor case of it, but Delilah's had worsened. Sara had gone with her aunt down to the nearest town. She'd sat on the front porch of Delilah's house and listened to her aunt and the doctor from the next town over argue over what medicine to give Delilah. In the end, none of it had worked. The infection had weakened Delilah and an unknown heart defect took her friend's life on a rainy May morning.

The town lost five children that year, but the one that Sara cared about the most was the smiling little girl who had loved her for being her. Sara had stood on the outskirts of the cemetery in a dress she'd found in an old trunk in the attic. It'd been the first and last time she ever wore one. After the service was over, Sara had sat down on the grass at the end of the fresh grave and cried. She'd held a bouquet of sage, peppermint, and eucalyptus in her hands from the small garden that she had planted in the woods.

Sara lifted a hand and wiped her damp cheek. She bowed her head and sniffed. She didn't know why she remembered Delilah now. It had been almost twenty years since her friend's death.

"Delilah developed pneumonia," Sara sniffed again and looked up at the sky overhead. She knew it wasn't real, but it gave her a sense of peace to see the blue sky and white clouds drifting by. "Her parents didn't know that she had a heart defect. By the time they realized it, it was too late. The doc from the next town over wouldn't listen to my aunt. He said that all her potions would do was make Delilah worse, but I knew better. My aunt knew her plants and their healing powers."

"How old was your friend?" Jaguin's deep voice asked.

Sara looked down to see her hand pressed against Jaguin's broad chest. Her fingers instinctively curled into the fabric of his shirt. She could feel the warmth of his skin through the material.

"Ten," she whispered, reaching up to brush another tear away only to pause when she felt his hand against her cheek. "She was so young."

"So were you to lose so much," Jaguin murmured.

Sara slowly lifted her head toward him. She stared into his eyes for several long seconds before her lips parted. Her fingers uncurled and she carefully ran her hand up his chest to his shoulder.

"Jaguin," she murmured, leaning closer to him. "I want to kiss you."

Jaguin reached for her other hand and pulled it against his chest. Sara glanced down at their joined hands. Hers looked so much smaller in his, yet she didn't feel afraid. Looking up at him again, she parted her lips and rose up onto her toes. She paused a brief second before sealing his lips with a tentative kiss that held a touch of hesitant wonder.

Chapter 8

Jaguin studied Sara's face as she gazed down at the leaf. He could see the dark circles under her eyes. She'd had another nightmare. He had instructed his symbiot to share them with him, but the symbiot had refused his request. At first, he'd been angry, but he quickly understood that it was loyal to Sara.

Still, if she continued to have them, he would have to insist that it comply with his wishes. If he was to help his mate, he needed to find the monsters in her dreams and slay them.

I wish we'd had just a few brief minutes with the bastard before Carmen killed him, Jaguin murmured heavily.

Me, too, his dragon agreed. *I go to her.*

Wait... Jaguin started to order before he released a frustrated groan.

I no wait. My mate need me, his dragon snorted in response, already beginning the climb down from the thick platform that looked like a large tree.

One of these days... Jaguin muttered.

That what Cree and Calo say to Carmen, his dragon retorted. *She just laugh at them.*

I know that is what they say, Jaguin snapped before he strained to focus on what his dragon was gazing at.

Jaguin was a little perturbed at his dragon. Its continued resistance to his control concerned him. He had never had this issue until recently. A part of him wanted to force his dragon to obey while another part was curious to see what it would do.

He silently lowered himself down to the floor and crept through the dense imagery of the holographic foliage. They both watched as Sara turned her face up toward the ceiling. Fascinated, he stepped out onto the path and took a step closer to her, mesmerized by the peaceful expression on her face.

He paused, one foot lifted to take another step, when she opened her eyes and turned her head to stare at him. He heard her swiftly inhaled breath and froze, unsure of what to do. His dragon trembled in anticipation of shifting should she appear scared.

I no hurt her, his dragon whispered.

I know, my friend, he replied in a soothing tone. *Give her time to get used to you.*

His heart pounded when he saw Sara take a step away from them. He could see the fear in her eyes, but he also saw curiosity. She tilted her head and stared at him for a moment.

"Jaguin! At least, I think it is you, unless you call your dragon something else," she exclaimed with a hint of confusion in her voice that changed to amusement when his dragon suddenly sat down and sneezed.

What are you doing? Jaguin asked in surprise at his dragon's behavior.

I give her time, his dragon stated, grinning at Sara with a goofy smile only a dragon could pull off.

A hiss escaped him when she stepped closer and raised her hand to touch his dragon. Her soft murmur teased his senses, washing through him and sending a wave of hope and excitement through him and his dragon. A moment later, he groaned in mortification when she started scratching him behind the ear and his dragon's leg thumped in response.

How are we supposed to impress her with you thumping like a Grombot with an itch? Jaguin muttered.

It feel good, his dragon retorted, thumping harder and emitting a deep purr of joy.

You are going to mess everything up! Jaguin started to say before he stopped when Sara began speaking again.

"I used to have an old hound dog that did the same thing when I scratched him there," Sara whispered in his ear. Her warm breath made his ear twitch and he held himself still when she continued to talk. "He was my best friend when I was ten. I grew up in the lower mountain area of the Appalachian Mountains."

Jaguin turned his head, his gaze following Sara as she pulled slightly away. He was pleased that she kept her hand on him. He could feel her fingers absently tracing the patterns of his scales as she spoke. It took a moment for him to comprehend that she was no longer talking about the dog she was comparing his dragon to, but about her life back on her world.

While she spoke in a calm, even tone, he could hear the sadness in her words. Her life had not been an easy one, but she still found humor in it. It wasn't until her voice dropped a notch that the true grief was evident. By the time the first tear slid down her cheek, he knew he needed to go to her.

Shifting, he reached for her. His heart squeezed with an unfamiliar emotion when he saw her eyes shimmer with tears. He pulled her close to his body and held her.

"How old was your friend?" He asked in a quiet voice.

"Ten," Sara whispered with a sniff and raised a shaky hand to wipe away the tear coursing down her cheek. "She was so young."

Jaguin listened to the tremble in her voice and lifted his hand to catch the tear. In the back of his mind, he raged that his mate had lived through so much sorrow and heartache. His own childhood had been happy and carefree in comparison. The only grief he ever dealt with was during the war. He lost several good friends during the various battles and could understand Sara's sorrow at the senseless deaths.

He tried to think of something to say when she stunned him again. Her words registered with his dragon before they did with him. A self-satisfied grunt resonated through him as his dragon settled down.

I tell you she like me, his dragon purred as all thoughts flew from Jaguin's mind and his body took over.

He deepened the kiss when Sara's lips parted. A shudder ran through him at the brief touch of her tongue against his. He wanted – needed – more. This is what he had been waiting centuries for, the touch of his mate.

Their tongues danced around each other, exploring the pleasure of their connection. He could feel her pulse quickening, yet he sensed that it wasn't from fear, but from desire. The feel of her hands sliding up his chest to his shoulders confirmed that she wanted this as much as he did.

His body hardened with desire. He had been with other women, but it had been to slake his lust. This was different. He could feel Sara's essence connecting with his symbiot and his dragon. Both of the other halves of him shimmered as the threadlike strands wove around them, making them one.

He moaned softly and tightened his arms around Sara's soft form, lifting her up against his body. His left hand slid down, cupping her buttocks as he did. Her legs instinctively opened to wrap around his waist. The position raised her until she was even with his lips. He pushed his hips forward when she started sliding down. He broke the kiss, breathing heavily as he gazed into her eyes.

"I need you, Sara," he admitted.

Sara gazed back at him, her face flushed with desire. At first, she didn't respond to his quietly spoken need. He didn't want to push her, she had been through so much, but he was also concerned about his own control. Being this close to her had been both pleasure and pain since she had first woken. Each time he left her, it became more difficult to walk away.

"Jaguin...," Sara started to say when her head turned at the angry hiss from the symbiot. "What's wrong?"

Jaguin heard the tremor in her voice and saw the flash of fear. His arms tightened around her and he sent a command to his symbiot to identify who had entered the room. Within seconds, he heard the familiar voices of Cree and Calo.

"It is the Twin Dragons and their mate," Jaguin murmured. "They are no threat."

"You'd better put me down before they see us," Sara whispered, blushing when she realized that she was still wrapped around him.

Jaguin scowled for a moment before he reluctantly lowered her to the floor, muttering a curse about killing the two warriors the next time they were alone. His lips twitched when he heard Sara's giggle at his frustrated remark.

"I really want you," he muttered with a lopsided grin.

"I can tell," Sara retorted, flushing when she felt his hard length pressed against her.

"Jaguin, our apologies," Calo called in greeting as he stepped onto the path. "Our mate wished to let her dragon out and the other rooms have a training exercise in progress."

* * *

Sara's eyes widened at the small green dragon that peeked over Calo's shoulder. Beside the tiny dragon, she saw Cree standing with a protective hand along her neck. She was the most beautiful creature Sara had ever seen – next to Jaguin.

"Who is that?" Sara asked, staring in awe at the dragon that was gazing back at her.

Calo's gaze softened and he turned toward the beautiful dragon. Raising his hand, he ran it tenderly along her jaw. Sara was amazed at how much love was in that simple gesture. She knew who the two warriors were; she'd seen them multiple times silently following Carmen. This was the first time she'd seen both men together. If it wasn't for the scar that Carmen had told her about and the way one of the men always had his hand on the knife by his side, she wouldn't have known there were two separate men watching Carmen.

"This is our mate, Melina," Calo introduced with a proud smile.

Sara's eyes widened further and she took a step back in surprise when the image shimmered for a moment before a young woman stood where the dragon was just seconds earlier. Cree immediately wrapped his arms around the woman when she swayed.

"Hi," Melina greeted, blushing and looking at Sara with curious, green eyes. "I'm sorry. My dragon wanted out and I'm still learning to do all this."

"You do not need to apologize," Cree growled, glancing at Sara and Jaguin with a sharp glance, warning them not to disagree.

Sara fought a grin when the woman rolled her eyes and mouthed to her not to listen to the big oaf. Sara gave a brief nod of understanding. She hesitantly pulled away from Jaguin and moved toward the woman. Her lips parted and she looked back and forth between Melina and the two huge men shadowing her.

"You look human," Sara said in a soft voice, gazing back at Melina.

"I am human," Melina replied with a shy smile. She raised a hand and pushed a strand of shoulder length dark brown hair behind her ear.

Sara frowned. "How can you transform into a dragon then?" She asked with a puzzled expression.

Sara felt Jaguin tense behind her. She laid her hand over his when his hand tightened on her hip.

"I'm not sure," Melina admitted. "I believe it has something to do with the Dragon's Fire that happens when…."

Sara saw Melina's face flame and her eyes sparkle as she looked back and forth between her mates. Understanding dawned quickly – something happened when the Valdier mated with a human to change the chemical composition of their bodies. If that happened, there would be no going back. Sara understood the dynamics of biology enough to know that once a species evolved, it rarely, if ever, returned to its previous state.

"Oh," Sara whispered.

"I'm sorry we interrupted you," Melina started to say, stopping when Sara gave her a brief smile.

"That's okay, we were just leaving," Sara replied. "Perhaps we can meet up later. Carmen and I were planning on meeting in the dining hall. She was going to show me more of the ship."

"That would be lovely," Melina replied, ignoring the soft growl from both her mates. "I think some girl time out would be wonderful."

Sara laughed when she saw the look of displeasure on Cree and Calo's faces and the soft grunt Jaguin emitted. It was obvious these guys had a lot to learn if they thought Earth girls were going to just sit around and wait to be escorted everywhere.

"I agree," Sara retorted, elbowing Jaguin when his hand tightened on her hip. "I'll see you in a few hours."

"Okay," Melina replied with a happy grin.

Sara pulled away from Jaguin and stepped around Melina, Cree, and Calo. She could feel Jaguin right behind her as she headed toward the door. A wave of warmth flooded her when she heard Melina's soft comment to the two men standing protectively near her.

"It is so nice to have other women close to my age here. I missed that when I was in the mining asteroid," Melina murmured.

She didn't hear the men's response. She would have to ask Melina what she meant about the mining asteroid. It was a clear reminder that Sara and Emma were not the only ones who had lived through horrible things. Carmen had almost died, something had happened to Melina, and Sara knew Audrey had a story behind her presence here as well.

Sara and Emma were so wrapped up in what happened to them that it was easy to forget to focus on the good that had come from their rescue. Unlike Emma, though, Sara had not been not a captive as long, had not witnessed as much of the cruelty, and did not have a family she cared for back home. Her family had not spoken to her since she'd left over ten years ago.

"Sara," Jaguin's voice drew her out of her own thoughts.

"Oh," she muttered, startled. "Sorry."

Jaguin gave her that lopsided grin she found endearing. She turned toward him, realizing they were already standing in front of the lift. At that moment, he looked like a little boy who was about to be told he wasn't going to get his favorite toy.

"I was hoping when you pressed your lips to mine…," he started to say before his voice died.

Sara tried to hide her smile, but failed. Her gaze softened when she saw his crestfallen expression. The humor of the situation wasn't lost on her, or the fact that if they hadn't been interrupted, their time together would have ended much differently. Raising her hand, she laid it on his chest.

"I enjoyed it," Sara said, not making any excuses. "I'm attracted to you, but I need to take this slowly. So much has happened…." For a moment, her gaze lowered to his chest where her hand rested as she thought about that fact. "Now, finding out what could happen if we... I'm not ready for this yet."

Jaguin raised his hand and covered hers, pressing it against his chest. She lifted her gaze and locked with his. His eyes had lost their twinkle of amusement and he stared back at her with an intense, serious expression.

"The change can only happen if I share my Dragon Fire with you. It would be very difficult to come together with you and not do so, but it is possible as long as I do not lose control of my dragon."

Jaguin paused a moment. "The human male... Did he....?" Jaguin pressed his lips together.

Sara knew what he was asking and shook her head. "No, Cuello wasn't sexually interested in us. He wanted to hurt us in a different way..." Sara's voice broke and she looked away. "I'd better get back to my room and check on Emma."

Jaguin released a deep sigh and nodded. "I will escort you," he said, reaching around her to wave his hand in front of the lift control. "But I warn you, my dragon and I will not give up."

Sara giggled when she saw his symbiot trotting down the corridor toward them in the shape of the jaguar. It was holding another stuffed sloth in its mouth. Shaking her head, she stepped into the lift.

"Neither will Honey," she chuckled.

"Honey?" Jaguin asked with a confused frown, turning to look at where she was staring. "You have named my symbiot Honey?"

"Unless you have a better name for it," she said.

Sara watched as Jaguin gave his symbiot a skeptical look. It stared up at him with a sharp-toothed grin, the sloth hanging by one foot from its mouth. The combination of the two powerful creatures staring at each other with a mixture of confusion, resignation, and flat-out goofy expressions was too much for Sara. She burst into a fit of giggles that soon had them all laughing.

Chapter 9

Jaguin scowled at Carmen. His gaze flickered between her face and what she was holding in her hand. Reaching out, he took the small box from her.

"How will this make her like me more?" He asked in confusion, staring down at the brightly wrapped package.

"It's chocolate. Sara mentioned earlier that one of the things she missed from Earth was the chocolate. I happen to have a lifetime supply thanks to Creon. I was having a major chocolate attack before we left. I don't know how he did it, but Creon had a ton of it delivered to Paul's ranch before we departed," Carmen explained.

"But... this was a gift from your mate," Jaguin said, frowning at Carmen. "You should keep this."

Carmen shook her head and pushed Jaguin's hand away. "Trust me, I have more than enough," she said with a smile. "Besides, I think Sara could use it more right now."

Jaguin looked skeptically at the package. "You are sure this will make her happy?" He asked, looking up at her face again.

Carmen chuckled and nodded. "Yes, trust me," she promised.

"Thank you," Jaguin responded, his expression clearing when he saw Creon walking toward them.

"Jaguin," Creon greeted. "How is your female doing?" He asked before he grunted when Carmen elbowed him in the stomach. "What?!"

"I'm not even going to tell you how condescending that sounds," Carmen retorted with a roll of her eyes. "That female has a name and it is Sara."

Creon grinned. "I know what her name is. I also knew I would get a reaction out of you," he teased, bending forward to brush his lips across hers before he wrapped his arms protectively around her waist. "I feel the girls moving. They are anxious to see the world."

"Not as much as I am to see them," Carmen murmured, turning in his arms and wrapping her own around Creon's neck.

Jaguin shook his head and turned to leave Carmen and Creon alone. It was obvious they had already forgotten his presence. He glanced down at the small package in his hand, turning it over thoughtfully as he walked toward the lounge that he now thought of as his and Sara's.

Carmen had stopped him to hand him the delicious treats just as he had stepped off the lift. He wasn't sure how they were supposed to break down the fragile barrier that Sara had tried to erect between them earlier. At this point, he was willing to try just about anything for another kiss.

He stepped into the room, frowning when he saw it was empty. Disappointment washed through him and he instinctively reached for the symbiot wrapped around his arm. He waited, staring out the window and turning the box over in his hands. He felt as nervous as a youngling waiting to sneak a quick peek at the girls visiting the village to see their first dragon races. He ran a hand through his hair.

So much for the fierce warrior, he thought in disgust. *I'm more like the….*

All thoughts deserted him when Sara suddenly appeared in the doorway. She gave him a nervous smile before stepping into the room. Jaguin swallowed and ran a damp palm along his pants leg.

"You look tired," he stated, wincing at his thoughtless words.

Sara released a self-conscious sigh and pushed her hair back from her face. She was wearing the blue cloth pants that she liked and a red blouse that hung loose around her. His brow furrowed when he noticed that she was wearing only socks.

"You have lost your shoes?" He asked, puzzled.

Sara chuckled. "No, I didn't lose my shoes, and yes, I'm tired. I'm still having difficulty sleeping," she admitted in a husky voice. "The memories… I can't seem to control them."

Jaguin's eyes darkened with concern. He opened his arms. Sara didn't hesitate. She stepped into his arms and hugged him in return. Her face turned into his broad chest. He felt the shudder go through her before she relaxed.

"Every time I think I have them under control, they hit me from out of nowhere," she whispered, rubbing her cheek against his shirt.

His arms tightened around her and he held her close. Closing his eyes, he ordered his symbiot to show him. This time, it must have understood he would not accept its refusal. Faint images, almost like shadows, danced in his mind before they solidified. He was seeing her thoughts, feeling her suffocating fear as the sound of footsteps echoed along the stone floor. The sound of metal on metal resonated through his mind before the first slash of pain tore through him. Almost as suddenly as it started, it stopped.

"Sara...," Jaguin whispered in a husky voice.

"Don't, Jaguin," Sara murmured, breathing heavily and holding him tight. "I don't want you to see it... to feel what it was like."

Jaguin pulled back and carefully lifted his hand to touch her chin. "Look at me, Sara," Jaguin ordered in a soft voice. "Look at me."

Sara reluctantly lifted her gaze to his. Her lips parted and she drew in a trembling breath as she stared up at him. He wanted her to see that she was not alone. He would never let her be alone again in the dark nightmares that held her captive.

"Trust me," he whispered, sliding his hand up along her cheek to cup it. "I have seen many things in my life. I have lived far longer than you, fought and watched those I care about die in a senseless war caused by those who crave power. You are no longer alone. Trust me to protect you."

Sara's eyes glistened with unshed tears. "I've never had anyone before," she admitted.

"You do now," he promised, drawing her closer. "You are my mate, my *elila*, my love. Give me your nightmares so that I may slay them."

"I'm… afraid," she finally choked out in a husky voice. "I'm afraid if I let them out, I'll never be able to capture them and put them back in the box. I'm not sure if I'm strong enough to survive it if I can't."

"I am strong enough," Jaguin assured her, leaning closer.

A single tear escaped to slide down Sara's cheek. The moment it struck his finger, he felt her let go of her nightmares. He drew in a deep breath as the suffocating fear returned a hundredfold. This time, the images weren't cast in the shadows, but in vivid, striking detail. The sight, sounds, and smells of the prison that Sara and Emma had been held in struck him with a savage blow. The painful memories would have sent him reeling if not for his determination to pull them away from Sara.

Agonizing pain ripped through him when he saw the brutality of Cuello and his men. It was not just the physical blows, but the mental ones that left scars no healer could see. He lived through Sara's abduction and the brutal murder of her friend and co-worker. The dark cloth over her head had not only blinded her, but made it difficult to breathe. She had fought to draw in each breath, afraid it would be her last. Her arms had been savagely twisted behind her and bound while the laughter of the men echoed in the vehicle they had placed her in.

"Oh, my *elila*, my precious mate," Jaguin groaned when he felt the first slash of the whip against her flesh.

Rage and sorrow fought with each other, threatening to drown him. Inside, he felt the strength of his mate – and her will to live. It was what made her who she was and his respect for her grew. Images from her childhood blended into her time in captivity. She thought of her aching loneliness after Delilah had died as well as running through the forest near her home to escape the taunts of her cousins. She also remembered the peace she had found in the plants she'd discovered and the small garden that she had grown deep within the woods.

He sorted through them, capturing the good memories and focusing on those so that they blossomed inside her and grew. He could never erase what she went through, but he could be there when they came and soothe her battered soul.

He moved his hand that was pressed against her cheek to thread his fingers through her hair. Her eyes were wide, haunted. Deep in their depths, he saw the frightened little girl and the brave, beautiful woman begging for help to protect her from the ravaging pain.

Hopelessness threatened to drown them, but he pushed through the choking memories. Instead, he surrounded her with warmth, love, and hope. His dragon rose up inside him, connecting with him and his symbiot, making them one as they battled the dark shadows of Sara's memories. His dragon roared, snapping and breathing fire at the inky shadows greedily reaching for her. His symbiot surged forward, wrapping Sara in golden armor that lit her mind with the memories of the beauty of her world. Through it all, Jaguin held her close to his body, his heart beating as one with hers, his mind and soul joined in a way that usually only happened after the Dragon Fire.

He scooped her into his arms when her knees gave out, cradling her and murmuring a soothing lullaby from his childhood. The deep chords encased her in the rhythm.

In the valley, the warrior stood.
As the battle drew close to home,
the warrior's shout mixed with blood.
The Great War had begun.
Warriors fought and won the fight,
but not all would live to go home.
In the valley, the warrior lay,
a blade thrust through his heart.
His dragon roared and his symbiot shimmered
as his life blood soaked into the soil.
The goddess heard his true mate's cry
and healed the thread that had severed.
In the valley, the warrior stood,
his true mate by his side.
Forever more they would be together.
A warrior and his mate watch frozen
as they stand guard and protect,
lest we forget the cost of war...

Jaguin sank down on the long sofa, holding Sara tightly to him as he sang. Slowly, the battle with the dark memories that had held her captive grew fainter. He continued to sing the chords that had been written by the sister of a grieving mate from his village shortly after the Great War had begun. He had known the warrior that died that day. It was his cousin and close friend. His grieving mate had knelt beside him, holding him and begging for the Goddess to heal the wound through her mate's heart.

Like the song, the Goddess had joined them together forever. Both his cousin and his cousin's true mate died that day. The people had erected a statue in the meadow where the battle took place, not far from the mountain village, to help remind those of the cost of war.

Jaguin's voice faded when he felt Sara's body relax. He raised his hand to tenderly brush a stray strand of her hair from her face before lightly tracing the curve of her jaw. A smile curved his lips at the peaceful expression on her face. Leaning down, he brushed a kiss across her forehead.

"Sleep, my mate. I will protect you," Jaguin whispered. "Even in your dreams, we will protect you."

Jaguin carefully switched the slightly crushed box in his left hand to his right. Leaning over, he placed it on the table beside them and leaned back. He would give her the treats tomorrow when she woke.

Settling back against the cushion, he gazed out the window into the darkness of space. He was a shadow in her mind now. Whenever the dark memories rose, he replaced them with the happy ones he had captured. He pushed away his own desire to strike out. There was no changing the past; they could only move forward. His eyes grew heavy, but his heart was light as he realized that Sara had given him a gift beyond measure. She had given him her trust.

"My precious, *elila*," he murmured, sleepily. "So brave, so beautiful, so fierce."

* * *

Far away, a golden figure stared into the swirling river of gold. The Valdier, Curizans, and Sarafin species considered her a goddess. She did not think of herself or her species as such. They were simply much older and had traveled vast distances through space and time, exploring, learning, and studying others.

On some worlds, they left a trace of their presence, while on others they were merely silent observers. They tried not to interfere if possible. It was not their way to command or change the course of a world. Yet, the more she studied this species and the new one her sisters had discovered, the more her curiosity grew.

Aikaterina watched the two figures in silence. Once again, this species drew something from deep inside her that she was unfamiliar with. Her fingers caressed the image of the two sleeping forms. Tiny strands of gold formed on each, adding a touch of her own blood to mix with the symbiot given to the warrior at birth. It was added protection to guard against the dark forces in the universe.

"I feel something, Aikaterina. You are well?" Arosa asked, settling down next to Aikaterina.

Aikaterina glanced up at the young figure of a woman. Arosa and her sister, Arilla, were very young for their kind. Aikaterina had discovered them among the stars and invited them to return to Valdier with her. Their species were few and far between. Many were lost among the stars.

"Yes, I am well," Aikaterina responded, looking down at the image of Jaguin and Sara.

Arosa tilted her head and stared at the two forms reflected in the river. "I like these species. There is something about them that makes them – different," Arosa said with a smile. "They make me feel warm inside."

"Yes, they do," Aikaterina murmured, not adding that they made her feel something else – a longing to understand what it meant when they talked of love. "There is something I must do," she said, floating upward.

"What? Do you need help?" Arosa asked, rising as well.

Aikaterina smiled serenely at Arosa and shook her head. "No," she stated, lightly floating over the uneven stones. "This I must do alone. I will not be gone long. Please make sure that you and your sister do not cause trouble while I am away."

"Who? Us?" Arosa teased, laying her hand against her shimmering chest.

Aikaterina raised an eyebrow, but didn't respond. Arosa and Arilla enjoyed spending time watching the human women that had come to this world. They also enjoyed getting into mischief. With a sigh, Aikaterina waved her hand. A doorway appeared before her. Through it, millions of star systems could be seen. Aikaterina flowed through the doorway.

"Where is she going this time?" Arilla asked her sister.

Arosa watched with a small smile. "I believe she is going back to the world of the human women," she replied.

"Does this mean we can go visit with Abby, Cara, Trisha, and Ariel?" Arilla asked with a hopeful expression.

"No," Arosa laughed. "Aikaterina just said we cannot cause trouble."

Arilla rolled her eyes. "Now, where is the fun in that?" She laughed as she began to fade.

Chapter 10

Sara woke sleepily, then froze when she felt a heavy weight holding her down. For a brief instant, fear held her paralyzed. Her eyes opened wide when she felt a shaft of warmth flood her. Almost immediately, her body relaxed – Jaguin, it was Jaguin's arm around her.

"We fell asleep again," she murmured, staring into his eyes.

His soft chuckle warmed her again, this time for a different reason. The guy was totally hot when he was just waking up. She could honestly say that was not the case with her last two lovers. His amused look vanished and a dark scowl creased his brow.

"Mm, you heard that thought, didn't you?" She murmured with a sheepish grin.

"Yes," he grunted with an unhappy look.

Sara raised her eyebrow at him. "Are you a virgin?" She asked with a pointed look.

A dark flush rose in his cheeks and he shifted uncomfortably. She caught brief flashes of a variety of different women. There were definitely more than her two previous relationships.

"No," he admitted with a slightly crooked grin.

"Enough said then," Sara muttered, pushing up to a sitting position before she winced. "Ugh, we need a bigger couch."

"Or a bed," Jaguin agreed, rolling his head to relieve the stiffness in his neck.

Sara glanced at him and chuckled. His hair was sticking up in several different directions, he had a couple days growth of beard on his face, and he was giving her a boyish look of hope. She shook her head and swung her legs over the side, pausing when she saw the slightly crumpled package on the table.

"What's this?" She asked, reaching for it.

"Chocolate. Carmen said it would make you happy," Jaguin replied.

"Chocolate?" Sara breathed out, gripping the package like it was a precious artifact. "I'm a total chocolate whore."

"I am not familiar with that term," Jaguin responded with a confused frown.

Sara released a happy sigh as she ripped open the package. She picked out a piece of chocolate and breathed in the delicious aroma before she bit into it. The bittersweet flavor of the dark chocolate combined with rich caramel washed over her taste buds sending a wave of pure bliss through her.

She turned and held out the other half to Jaguin who instinctively opened his mouth to sample the tasty tidbit. His eyes widened at the explosion of flavor. He slowly chewed on it, understanding Carmen and Sara's enjoyment of the delicate treat. It was almost as good as the tasty Maratts and Grombots. Both were considered a rare, delicious delicacy to Valdier dragons.

"There is no such thing as too much chocolate," Sara stated, reaching for another one. "Or coffee."

"Coffee?" Jaguin asked as he picked up another piece of the chocolate, this one in a different shape.

"Coffee has caffeine and is great for waking you up and giving you an energy boost to help keep you going," Sara explained with a chuckle.

Jaguin released a slight shudder. "I do not think it would be good for Lord Trelon's mate to have such a thing. She moves very quickly, all the time, and gets into everything even without it. You will get to meet her. She is very tiny. She reminds me of a Maratt; very fast and hard to catch. I will ask her if she can program this treat into our replicators. Then you will have as much of it as you wish."

Sara laughed. "I'll end up the size of a house if you do that," she retorted with a sigh as she picked up her third piece. "Thank you, Jaguin."

"For what?" He asked, a puzzled frown creasing his brow.

Sara's gaze softened. "For being you," she replied, leaning forward to brush a light kiss across his lips.

Jaguin's expression cleared and he raised his hand to tenderly run it down Sara's cheek. She turned her face into his warm palm, enjoying the rough texture. She had never been a real touchy-feely girl, but there was something about this strange alien male that she connected with.

"I have to report for duty soon," he murmured. "I will meet you here later."

Sara turned her gaze to his face. She nodded. He rose to his feet and held his hand out to her. She placed her hand in his and stood up. For several long seconds, they stared at each other.

"Sara," he started to say.

"Jaguin," she whispered at the same time before clearing her throat and smiling. "You go first."

"I... Last night...," he paused and ran his hand through his hair. "I wanted you to know that last night meant a great deal to me. You are one of the bravest females I have met."

Sara shook her head. "No, not brave," she murmured, lowering her gaze. "I was very, very frightened. I still am."

She lifted her head when he gently slid his hand up to cup her chin. "You are to me," he said, leaning down to brush a kiss across her upturned lips. "I am glad the goddess led me to you."

Sara watched as he pulled back and straightened. Her fingers trembled as they rose to touch her lips. She could still feel the warmth of his lips against them. She felt another piece of the fragile wall she had built around her heart crumble at his sincere words.

Stepping silently through the door, he murmured that he would meet her later. He lifted the hand he was holding to his lips and pressed a hot kiss full of promise against the back of it. Sara watched him turn and stride down the long corridor toward the lift at the far end. Her gaze moved down to the box of chocolate in her left hand after he disappeared from sight.

"I'm falling in love with him," she whispered in shock. "What am I going to do?"

Her gaze lifted to stare down the empty corridor. She had cared for the men in her other relationships, but the wall around her heart had been firmly in place and she'd never really let them get close to her. She had been sad when the relationships ended, but she had also been ready. This... This was different. This wasn't just about companionship. This was about forever.

Sara blinked and turned when the lift opened and two warriors stepped out. She quickly retreated to her quarters. She needed time to think. Time to decide what path she wanted her life to take – a future where she would be able to return to her life back on Earth or an unknown future on an alien world.

* * *

Sara slowed as she stepped into the lounge later that evening. Jaguin was already there, standing next to the window. He appeared to be deep in thought.

Sara pushed down the overwhelming desire to walk over and wrap her arms around him. She could feel a distance between them, as if there was a wall between them. It took a moment for Sara to realize that wall had been there for a few hours now, and it was coming from her. It was the same type of wall she always built between her and the world, she had just never recognized it before.

"Hi," she said, pushing her hands into the front pockets of her jeans.

She watched as Jaguin drew in a deep breath. He didn't turn around to greet her; instead, he continued to look out into space.

"You can fight your feelings for me, Sara, but it will not change them," Jaguin said in a quiet voice.

"How...? Oh," she said, fingering the symbiot on her wrist.

Jaguin slowly turned to face her. His face was drawn, but his eyes glittered with determination. Sara looked away from the heated gaze.

"I didn't realize..." she started to say before her voice faded.

"We connected last night, Sara, in a way that usually happens only between true mates after the Dragon's Fire is completed. We became one. I know your thoughts as you would know mine if you wished," Jaguin said in a slow, even tone. "You cannot deceive me, Sara. I know your true feelings."

Sara swallowed and drew in a deep breath. She had not been not expecting this. The carefully crafted speech she had planned to tell him flew from her mind at his softly spoken words. Inside, she flinched. She felt raw, exposed.

"Sara," Jaguin muttered in a raw voice. "Give us a chance."

"I can't," Sara whispered, finally looking up at him. "You know why. You know... I'm not like other women. I'm not made for a long-lasting relationship. I don't... I can't fall in love with you."

"I won't hurt you or turn away from you, Sara. I am not like your aunt or cousins. I won't leave you the way Delilah or your mother did, and I will never take you for granted," Jaguin said in a soft voice.

Sara's chin lifted and she locked her jaw to keep it from trembling. Her arms wrapped around her waist and she curled her fingers into a fist to keep them from reaching out to him.

"My home...," she whispered, staring at him when he shook his head and took a step toward her.

"Is now on Valdier, with me," he said with a quiet certainty that shook her.

This time it was Sara's turn to shake her head. She stared at him. She had fought with her own emotions all afternoon. The turning point had been when she'd realized the power she had given Jaguin over her when she had opened herself to him. When she was a child, she'd promised herself she would never do that again after her mom, in one of her rare visits, had showed up for the last time. Selma Wilson had brushed off the grieving ten-year-old little girl as if she were an irritating insect.

Sara had opened her heart and her mother had torn it out and stomped on it. Her aunt had been almost as bad, telling Sara that she should be thankful she wasn't lying next to Delilah. When Sara had cried out that she wished she were, her aunt had looked coldly at her and said that at least it would be one less mouth to feed.

That coldness had sunk deep into Sara's soul, freezing her heart and giving her the strength to set off on her own path without looking back. Jaguin's connection last night had broken through that wall she had built, showing that she was still the raw, fragile girl deep inside with the same fears and uncertainty.

"I can't," Sara whispered, shaking her head and breaking contact.

She stiffened when Jaguin stepped closer to her. She stared down at the tips of his boots. She didn't look up at him and he didn't touch her. He didn't have to as long as she wore his symbiot. He could feel the pain threatening to rip her apart.

"I will not give up, Sara," Jaguin swore.

"Why? Why?" She asked in a small, confused voice.

"Because once a Valdier warrior has found his true mate, he will do everything in his power to protect her, even if it is from her own fears," he said before he stepped out of the room.

Sara's shoulders trembled and she bit down hard on her bottom lip to keep the cry of pain from escaping. Tears streamed down her face and she struggled to draw in a breath. The pain was almost physical in its intensity.

She shuddered when the door behind her opened. Her vision blurred when Honey sat down in front of her and gazed up at her with a woeful expression. One of her small stuffed sloths hung by an arm from its mouth.

"Oh, Honey," Sara whispered in a trembling voice. "Why does life have to hurt so much?"

The huge golden Werecat pushed the stuffed animal into her hand. Sara wiped at her eyes and grasped the sloth. She hugged it to her and walked over to the couch. A moment later, she and Honey were curled up on the couch. Sara's arms were wrapped around the soft fabric animal while Honey lay with her head on Sara's lap.

Chapter 11

Jaguin swung the heavy battle sword again and again. The two men he fought slowly backed away from the savage blows. It was only when he whirled around and knocked Creon off his feet, pinning him to the ground with the blade that he backed off.

Sweat dripped from all three men and they were breathing heavily from the fight. Creon finally rolled to his feet and straightened as he drew in a deep breath.

"Program end," Creon called out in a loud voice before turning to glare at Jaguin.

The thick forest around them faded as the computer shut down the training program. Gunner stared warily at Jaguin as he touched the corner of his lip. He grimaced when he saw the blood from where Jaguin had struck him.

"I haven't seen you this mad – ever," Gunner muttered, waiting as his symbiot healed the numerous cuts and bruises on his body.

"This is a training session, not a mission to kill," Creon retorted, wiping an arm across his brow. "You have become more and more volatile over the last week. I had *hoped* that a challenging workout would help calm you, but there is only one thing I can think of that could cause this type of aggression: you are losing control of your dragon. What is wrong? You have a true mate, you shouldn't be having this type of control issue."

Gunner grimaced again and stared with a glum expression at Jaguin. "It must be the human female. Having a true mate is no guarantee that it will calm our dragons, especially if they don't accept us," he replied, sinking to the floor of the training room. He glanced at Creon with a wry look. "You should have warned us that human females could be this difficult," he added with a sigh as he leaned forward and rested his arms on his knees, his gaze turned toward Jaguin.

Jaguin rolled his shoulders. He was still lost in the haze of battle and fighting for control of his dragon. Once again, he felt close to the edge of darkness. His dragon strained to get out. Rage, despair, and grief twisted through him. He wanted, needed, his mate.

"Jaguin," Creon warned, reaching out and gripping Jaguin's arm in a strong, unbreakable grip. "Focus."

"I… am… trying," Jaguin bit out through gritted teeth. "It is my dragon. He is…."

"Calm him," Creon ordered.

Jaguin drew in a deep breath. The scales of his dragon moved over his skin. He could feel the angry beast straining to get free. He lowered himself to one knee and breathed deeply, focusing on calming the primitive creature that was his other half.

You must calm, my friend, Jaguin soothed.

Mate hurting. I go to her, his dragon snarled savagely.

If you do not calm, it will not be safe enough for either of us to go near her, Jaguin replied, reaching deep to calm the pain of his dragon. *We cannot give up yet. I know she needs us. We must give her time.*

No more time, his dragon snapped, whipping around.

Jaguin felt the thin thread he had held on to between him and his dragon disintegrate. The hissing breath that he'd started to release changed to a roar as his dragon took control. The sounds of Creon and Gunner's yells of warning echoed as if from a vast distance as he shifted. A red haze settled over him. His only thought was to go to his mate.

"Jaguin!" Creon snarled, his own body shimmering as he tried to get through the fog of pain radiating outward. "Take back control."

Jaguin swung around, his tail snapping out with a deadly force at Creon. Creon saw the movement and dove to the side, shifting into his dragon as he did. Gunner rolled and transformed as well. Jaguin jerked around, snapping at the other dragon.

I order you to stand down, Creon hissed in the language of the dragons.

I go to mate, Jaguin's dragon snapped back, refusing to back down. *Mate hurting.*

She needs you, Gunner agreed. *But, not like this.*

I take her. She mine! Jaguin snarled.

Take control, Creon growled.

Jaguin charged Gunner, hitting him in the chest. Deep gouges formed on the metal floor as the impact forced Gunner to scramble for footing. His back left leg buckled and he fell to the floor.

Jaguin took advantage of the other dragon's vulnerability. His front left foot landed on Gunner's neck, holding him down as he prepared to strike. Gunner struggled to break free.

Jaguin, Gunner choked out.

Jaguin's savage snarl echoed through the room for a brief moment before it was cut off when Creon wrapped his tail around Jaguin's neck and pulled him back with enough force to send him flying through the air. Jaguin flipped in midair and landed on his feet almost ten feet away.

Creon stepped between him and Gunner. Jaguin's mind was burning with an intense rage. His tail flicked back and forth as his gaze moved over the two males standing between him and the exit to the room. Reaching forward, he dragged his front right claw along the metal. The loud screeching sound echoed through the room, a furious warning to them both.

Jaguin, stand down or I will make you, Creon warned in a deadly voice.

The heated response of Jaguin's dragon died in his throat when the door to the room opened. The red glow intensified as two figures hurried into the room. His front leg reached out again, his head lowered, and his gaze locked on the figure staring back at him in shock.

"Carmen, get out of here! He is out of control," Creon ordered, shifting back to his two-legged form.

Carmen stopped, her right hand going protectively to her abdomen while her worried gaze moved back and forth between her mate and Jaguin's enraged dragon. She started to step backwards, waving with her other hand for Sara to retreat through the open door.

The fire in Jaguin's eyes flared again and he took advantage of Gunner and Creon's distraction to attack. Striking swiftly, he wrapped his tail around Creon's legs and jerked him off the ground. He tossed Creon's body up in the air and swung around to slice his claws across Gunner's exposed chest before returning his attention to Creon's falling body.

"No!" Carmen screamed.

Creon shifted again into his dragon as he dropped to the floor. Jaguin twisted around and his tail swung outward to protect him from the dragon rushing toward him. He curled the end around the slender column of Carmen's neck. Creon and Gunner froze. Jaguin held the female dragon for a split second before he released her and spun around.

Jaguin pushed back the black form of Creon's dragon. Gunner shifted back to his two-legged form. Jaguin ignored both of them as he moved to the far corner of the room.

A shudder ran through Jaguin's large frame. The pain ripping through his dragon was heart-wrenching. He had come very close to killing Carmen. Attacking a female dragon, especially one heavy with child, was an unspeakable act for a Valdier warrior.

"Carmen, are you hurt?" Creon's husky voice echoed loudly in the sudden silence of the room.

"I'm fine," she replied. "Jaguin...."

"He has lost control of his dragon. He will have to be confined until a decision can be made," Creon responded.

"What kind of decision?" Sara asked in a soft, slightly uneven tone.

"Whether he should be given the mercy of death or confined for the rest of his life. A dragon out of control, especially one as powerful and deadly as Jaguin's, can leave a path of devastation," Creon replied in a grim voice.

Jaguin didn't turn. He knew Creon was right. He was dangerous. Pulling away from the others, he focused on his grieving dragon.

Calm, my friend. I know your pain. It is mine as well, Jaguin murmured in a soothing tone.

I no good for our mate, his dragon grieved.

It is just as well she turned away from us before it was too late. The weight of what happened is not only on you. My own feelings are tied to yours. What happened could not have transpired if my own anger had not magnified your own, Jaguin replied in a tone filled with remorse.

I no want to live without mate, his dragon informed him in a mournful tone.

Jaguin released a tired sigh. As much as he hated to admit it, his dragon's behavior had shown him that the fragile hold he had on his other half was too frayed to mend. He was a danger to everyone – including his own mate.

* * *

"Sara, go to him," Carmen urged, recognizing the pain in Jaguin's eyes.

"Carmen," Creon started to warn before he hesitated and glanced at Sara. "Be careful, Sara. If he tries to attack, understand that Gunner and I will do whatever is necessary to protect you."

"He won't hurt me," Sara whispered, staring at Jaguin. "I'd... I would like to be alone with him. Please...," she added, glancing at Creon and Gunner with a pleading look.

Sara watched as Creon opened his mouth to protest only to close it and nod when Gunner touched Creon's arm and shook his head. Worry darkened his eyes, but Sara knew deep down that Jaguin would never hurt her. She turned when the door opened again and Honey quietly entered. The intense sadness in the symbiot's gaze tore at her. The last week had been sheer torture. Swallowing, Sara waited until the other three left, leaving Sara, Honey, and Jaguin alone.

Drawing in a deep breath to steady her nerves, Sara quietly walked across the large room to where the dragon stood. A tentative smile curved her lips when she saw it glance at her quickly before looking away. In that brief glance, she'd caught the intense sadness. Her heart wrenched at the thought of hurting something so beautiful.

A startled gasp escaped her when Jaguin suddenly shifted. One moment, she was focused on the dragon, the next she was staring into the dark, troubled eyes of the man. Sara paused, unsure of what to do or say.

"You shouldn't be here. It is not... safe," Jaguin stated in a sharp tone.

Sara tucked her hands into the front pockets of her jeans and stared back at him in silence. He looked tired. He also looked like he had lost some weight. He wasn't the only one. She knew she looked just as tired and the little weight she had gained had evaporated. Tandor had been giving her lectures on it almost daily.

"You won't hurt me," Sara replied with a wry confidence.

"My dragon might," Jaguin bit out in a husky tone.

Sara shook her head. "No, he won't," she said in a soft voice. "What happened? Creon seems to think you're out of control."

"I am," Jaguin snapped, lifting his hands to run them through his hair in aggravation. "I can't control my dragon any longer. When a warrior gets to that point, it is too dangerous to allow him to live."

"So, just because of a little loss of control, you think you should be executed?" Sara asked in disbelief.

Jaguin shook his head and tiredly ran a hand down his face. He dropped his hand down to his side and turned away from her. Sara was shocked by the slight droop in Jaguin's powerful shoulders.

"It is for the best, Sara. A warrior craves a mate to call his own, but a dragon... A dragon needs his mate to survive. The loneliness eats at him. You have to understand, for him to know he has a true mate, but never to claim her... Death would be more merciful."

Sara scowled at Jaguin's back. Her lips tightened and she clenched her fists for a moment as her mind raced wildly to process what he was saying. It was ludicrous to give up so easily. Reaching out, she touched Jaguin's arm. He immediately stiffened. His shoulders rolled and she could feel the muscles under her fingers flex.

"Change back," she ordered.

Jaguin slowly turned toward her, his eyes filled with surprise. "What?" He asked warily.

Sara gave him an intense stare. "I want to talk to your dragon. I need you to change back into him," she said.

Jaguin shook his head. "Sara, I do not believe that is wise," he responded, taking a step back so that she couldn't touch him again. "I barely have him under control. The only reason I do is because of his remorse at almost killing Carmen. If I let him out again, I'm not sure I will be able to restrain him."

Sara gazed back at Jaguin with a calm, determined gaze. She wanted – needed – him to know that she wasn't afraid of him or his dragon. She also wasn't going to stand by and allow Jaguin to just end his life. She wasn't ready to move their relationship forward yet, but that didn't mean she wasn't working on it.

"Change back, Jaguin," Sara whispered, stepping forward. "I need to talk to him."

"Sara...," Jaguin's guttural groan filled the room at her pleading gaze. "I will do what I can to keep him under control. If… If I can't, you have to promise you will get out of here as quickly as you can." His gaze moved to his symbiot where it sat watching them in silence. "You must protect her at all cost, do you understand?"

The symbiot's head bowed in acknowledgement and its body shimmered. Sara took several steps back when Jaguin shot her a look of warning.

Her lips parted in wonder when Jaguin closed his eyes and released a deep breath. His body shimmered, much like the symbiot, as he transformed. Sara's eyes softened when she saw the hesitant look in the dragon's eyes as it looked at her before quickly looking away.

"Jaguin," Sara murmured, stepping closer. "Hey, big guy. I see you're having a bit of a rough time."

The large silver body shivered before the dragon turned back to gaze at her. Twin flames burned in its eyes, but for some reason, Sara didn't feel worried about it. She gave the dragon a rueful look and reached out to touch one nostril. Her hand paused when the dragon jerked its head away and turned from her.

Sara watched as the dragon moved away from her. Ten feet away, it glanced back at her before it turned away and lay down. Sara sighed and her heart melted when it stretched its long neck out and rested its chin on the hard metal floor. She slowly walked forward. Stopping next to Jaguin, she released another long sigh and sank down onto the floor next to his head. She didn't touch him. Instead, she drew her legs up, wrapped her arms around them, and rested her chin on her knees.

"I'm so sorry. I didn't mean to hurt you," she began in a soft voice. With a low groan, she buried her face against her knees. "I'm so screwed up right now I don't know what to do."

Tears burned her eyes. She knew she needed to get her own life sorted before she could deal with anything else. She was still having the horrible nightmares. Those, combined with having to open her mind and deal with her own baggage before her captivity, had left her feeling shattered, confused, and second-guessing her decisions until now. Sara angrily wiped the moisture from her eyes and lifted her head. The dragon was staring back at her with such a woeful expression that Sara couldn't contain the dry laugh that escaped her.

"We're a mess, aren't we?" She asked in a somber tone. "Me with my insecurities and demons, and you with your...." She shook her head, unsure of what to call it – mate problems? "I just need a little time to think things through. You know, sort them out. I miss our time together, it's just... I need to figure all this out."

Sara slid her legs down when the dragon nudged her arm. She scooted closer and wrapped her arms around Jaguin's broad head. Leaning forward, she pressed a kiss to his brow and sighed. Her fingers absently caressed his right ear.

"So, what made you all huffy and puffy earlier?" She asked in a soft voice.

A giggle escaped her when Jaguin blew a smoke ring and snorted. A long series of low rumbles, growls, and snorts escaped Jaguin. Sara could tell he was talking to her. She hummed and hawed as if she understood him, nodding when he paused and looked at her before he continued. She felt like she was Pete listening to Elliott the dragon. All that was needed was for him to disappear on her or toast a few apples while she burst out into song.

Almost ten minutes passed before the dragon finally became quiet again. Something told Sara that even Jaguin was surprised by his dragon's behavior. She continued scratching him behind the ear, laughing when his back leg thumped when she hit the 'magic' spot as she liked to think of it. She grimaced when he stared back at her in silence, knowing it was her turn to share.

"I'm not so sure this is really a fair conversation," she mumbled, tracing his left brow with her fingers. "You make me feel things I've never felt before. I've had two previous relationships, each ending in disaster when the guys felt more for me than I felt for them." Sara's fingers paused when Jaguin emitted a soft growl. She looked him in the eye and raised an eyebrow. "Do you want to hear this or not? If you don't, I'll take my unhappy ass back to my room. If this is going to work, you need to listen to me rumble and growl, too."

Sara waited until Jaguin released another snort before he lowered his head and rested his chin on her lap. A reluctant smile tugged at her lips. She wouldn't admit it, but this was a first. In her previous relationships, she would have just walked out without bothering to explain why, and she would have kept going.

"Where was I?" She murmured, frowning as she tried to pick up where she left off.

Jaguin emitted a series of rumbles and snorts as if he was repeating what she had said. Sara was surprised when faint images of her life before flashed through her mind. She glanced warily at where Honey lay watching them from a few feet away.

"This is definitely the strangest conversation I've ever had," she muttered with a roll of her eyes. "So, I was in two previous relationships, neither worked out. I realize now that I was just lonely and they were safe because I knew I'd never love them. Well, the first one was safe, the second one – not so much, but that is a different story." Sara glanced down with a skeptical look. "Are you sure you really want to hear all this?"

Jaguin's head nodded just a tad. Sara groaned. He wasn't going to let her get distracted. Drawing in a deep breath, she focused on what she was trying to tell him.

"I told you a little about my childhood. It wasn't all that great. I know there is such a thing as a happy relationship between two people, Delilah's parents had that before she died, but, well, that kind of relationship seemed to be pretty few and far between where I grew up. It just seemed like a lot of work for something that wasn't likely to happen. My real mom, she never gave two cents on a pig's tail what happened to me. My aunt wasn't much better, though she kept me from going to a foster home, so I figure in the long run I was better off. Life wasn't easy, but it wasn't impossible. I know I have abandonment issues. I'm working on those. It's the other issues...." Sara shook her head and lowered it. "I need time, that's what I'm really trying to say. I just need time to deal with my past, my present, and figure out what I want in my future. I'd like to spend more time with you, in this form as well, if you don't mind. Maybe that will help us both. I'll get used to being in an alien world, still get to spend time with you without feeling all nervous, and figure out what in the hell I'm talking about. God! So much for having a Ph.D.! This is so messed up I don't even understand myself."

Sara groaned and buried her face against Jaguin. A moment later, she felt the warmth of Honey as the symbiot shifted into a large three-toed sloth and wrapped his long arms around her. They sat there for a long time, just holding each other.

Before Sara knew it, she was slowly sliding down as exhaustion from lack of sleep, her emotional confession, and the adrenaline dump from Carmen's frantic command to follow her earlier washed over her. She snuggled up against Jaguin when he rolled onto his side and wrapped his wing around her, pulling her closer to him. Her fingers spread wide, trying to touch as much of him as she could. Honey slid under her, forming a soft bed.

"You know, I could get used to this," Sara mumbled sleepily. "Do you think anyone would mind if we just crashed here for a little while?"

Jaguin's side moved as he chuckled. Sara's soft, sleepy laugh mixed with his. She looked over her shoulder when the room grew dim. The room was no longer empty. Instead, they were in the forest again. This time it was night and the sky was filled with the brilliant luminous sparkle of millions of stars. All around them, trees and large plants rose up, some with glowing flowers larger than a dinner plate nestled among the sights, scents, and sounds of the forest. In the distance, Sara could hear the sound of a stream.

"It's so beautiful," Sara whispered, afraid to break the magic of the program. "I wish it were real. I could lose myself in it."

Jaguin's wing tightened around her and his head rose to look up at the stars. From the angle where she was lying, Sara could see the proud profile of the dragon. Curling her fingers around the edge of his wing, she held it to her – feeling safer than she ever had in her life.

* * *

I tell you she like me better than you, his dragon purred, holding Sara close to his body.

She does not, Jaguin muttered. *She just isn't ready to accept her feelings for us yet.*

She accept me, his dragon argued. *She talk to me.*

She was talking to me, too, Jaguin pointed out. *We are one and the same, in case you have forgotten.*

We stay in this form, his dragon replied. *She accept this form.*

And how are we supposed to give her the Dragon's Fire if you don't let me out? Jaguin asked in exasperation. *Have you forgotten that? If you want your mate, we have to work together to get Sara to accept us both.*

I not think of that, his dragon muttered.

You also need to keep your temper. Another outburst like you did earlier and Lord Creon won't hesitate to put us both out of our misery.

I not mean to. Our mate hurting. I want to go to her, his dragon snorted.

I know, my friend, but we are both too close to the edge. We need to be careful – for Sara's sake as well as our own, Jaguin gently reproached.

I be good, his dragon said with remorse. *I not try to kill the others no more.*

Thank the goddess for that, Jaguin retorted before he released a tired sigh. *Watch over her.*

I will, his dragon promised. *I always protect mate.*

Chapter 12

Two weeks later, Sara stared down at the planet that would be her and Emma's home for the foreseeable future. It was different from Earth in some ways, and yet similar in others. She turned when Emma walked up to stand beside her.

"It's beautiful," Sara commented, turning to stare back down at the planet.

Emma nodded. Sara wound an arm around the other girl's waist and tilted her head to rest it against Emma. They stood like that for a long time, not speaking.

"Tandor wants... to see us... before we... leave," Emma forced out in a soft, trembling voice.

Sara frowned and stared moodily down at the planet again. Tandor had been checking in daily to make sure that they were eating. Sara was, but she worried about Emma. The other woman was becoming more withdrawn the closer they got to the planet.

Sara straightened and wrapped her arms around her waist. The past two weeks had been a mixture of ups and downs for her emotionally. The realization that she had opened herself up to Jaguin in a way that left her vulnerable and defenseless had scared the hell out of her. Sometimes...well, Emma wasn't the only one who wanted to hide.

The *Horizon* had become a small world of its own; and, while she couldn't speak for Emma, Sara had grown accustomed to living on it. Staring down at the planet below forced her to realize that all of this was real. The planet represented a new unknown. A strange world where aliens lived and dragons ruled.

She wasn't going to admit that she would never see Earth again. Someday she might even know whether or not she wanted to see it again. For now, she was firmly not thinking about it.

The past two weeks had been crazy. It had taken a few days for Creon to relax the protective guard he had assigned to Jaguin. The fact that it hadn't been necessary to protect anyone from Jaguin's dragon helped Creon to eventually believe Jaguin's assurances that he had his dragon under control again, thanks to Sara's help. Sara grimaced. Creon had ordered her to spend at least an hour a day with Jaguin's dragon.

"It is for all of our sakes," Creon had told her. "I will do whatever it takes to protect my people. Jaguin is a great warrior and a good friend. I have no wish to end his life, but I will if he becomes a threat to others."

"Isn't that a little harsh?" Sara remembered asking in astonishment. "Surely something less drastic could be done."

Creon had shaken his head. "A Valdier warrior is not like a human one, Sara. A male dragon out of control can devastate a village. No warrior wants to live with that guilt."

"It just seems so... cruel," Sara had responded with a shiver.

"There are worse things in life than death, Sara," Creon had replied.

Sara remembered the brief flash in Creon's eyes. Something told her that he was speaking from experience. It had shaken her to see such powerful men vulnerable.

In the end, Sara found she looked forward to spending time with Jaguin in his dragon form. They would meet in the large room each evening. Jaguin would greet her in his two-legged form, as she had come to think of it, before he shifted. The first few times, she'd noticed he appeared agitated. When she had asked what was wrong, he had replied in a short, clipped tone.

"My dragon is very impatient," he had muttered with a grimace.

"Oh."

Sara had to admit that she was more comfortable with the dragon then she was with the man. Her face heated and she could feel her body react to the reason why – she wanted Jaguin and it was becoming more difficult to deny that, especially to herself.

Sara returned to the present when Emma stiffened and turned to face the door when it opened. She turned as well, watching as Tandor entered the room. A small, nervous smile curved her lips at his assessing gaze.

Sara sighed; she swore that Tandor must be a closet psychic. If he wasn't, he gave a pretty damn good impression of it. Personally, she was more worried about Emma than herself. Sara *was* still struggling to come to terms with everything that had happened – and what her future would look like – but Sara liked to think she was stronger than most due to the way she grew up. From the little Emma had shared, her upbringing had been completely different than Sara's. The surprise child of two parents later in life, Emma had been sheltered and loved.

"Are you two ready to go down to the planet?" Tandor asked with a soothing smile.

"Yes, I'm excited to get off the ship! Nervous, too," Sara replied with an anxious smile, tucking her hair back behind her ear. "The ship is really cool and all, but I'm not used to being cooped up in one spot for so long. I'm curious to see if some of the things Jaguin showed me are real. I've spent most of my life running wild. This has been the equivalent of caging a fox in a hen house! I'm ready to start chasing a few chickens if I don't get off this thing."

Emma giggled and turned when a reflection appeared in the window. Sara's laughter mixed with Emma's when she saw what had captured her friend's attention. The symbiot had divided into smaller sections and now a dozen or more golden hens were strutting around the room.

They were both laughing at the antics of the chickens when the door to their room chimed. Sara called out for whoever was on the other side to enter. She crumbled into another fit of giggles when Jaguin stepped inside. He came to a sudden stop when the miniature golden chickens suddenly surrounded him.

"What the….?" Jaguin muttered in shock, gazing down when one of the creatures pecked at his boot. "My symbiot has gone mad," Jaguin exclaimed in dismay.

"No, it hasn't," Sara laughed with a shake of her head. "I was telling Emma and Tandor that I was feeling like a fox in a hen house." Jaguin looked at her in confusion. Sara shook her head again and waved her hand. "Never mind. Tandor was asking if we were ready to go down to the planet."

Tandor nodded, looking warily as several hens walked toward him. "Lady Carmen thought it wise to check on you before we departed. She has refused to use the transporter and wishes to return via a shuttle. She thought you both might like to join her and Lord Creon."

Sara didn't miss the way Tandor's gaze swept over Emma. They were all worried about the delicate woman. Sara smiled and nodded, turning to Emma, who was watching with silent hesitation.

"I don't remember much about how we got on board the ship, but the idea of being reduced to the smallest particle and put back together is not something I would particularly like to try while I'm coherent. Do you know where we'll be staying when we get down to the planet?" Sara asked in curiosity as Tandor stepped forward with the familiar scanner that he carried.

"You'll be a guest at the palace," Jaguin said with a glance at his symbiot which had reformed into the familiar jaguar that Sara liked.

"At the... Wow! That will be a first," Sara muttered, glancing at Emma with a raised eyebrow. "I wonder if they will have singing teapots and dancing silverware to go along with the dragons?"

Emma's lips twitched, and for a moment her eyes lost the sad, confused look in them as if she was remembering happier times. Sara turned back to Tandor when he stepped back and glanced down at the scanner. His gaze flickered to Emma with a worried expression before he nodded to Jaguin.

"Everything appears to be fine," Tandor informed them. "I have several things to do before I depart. Jaguin will escort you both to the transport."

Sara watched as Tandor turned and exited the room. She drew in a deep breath. This was it, another adventure. The breath she was holding squeezed out when she looked up at Jaguin. He was watching her with an intense gaze that drew an immediate reaction from her.

"Are you ready?" He asked in a deep voice that sent a shiver through her.

Sara knew immediately there was more to that question; he also wanted to know if she was ready to accept the growing feelings between them. Her heart pounded as she thought about the last few months. He had been her constant companion, someone that she could lean on when the dark fears threatened to drown her.

"Yes, I... I think I'm ready," she whispered, unable to look away.

She started when she heard a sound to the left. Blinking, she pulled her gaze away to see Emma standing in the doorway holding two small bags. An appreciative smile curved her lips and she walked over and took the bags containing her clothes and personal belongings. A frown creased her brow when she saw the enormous collection of stuffed animals piled on her bed.

"What about my sloths?" Sara asked, looking up at Jaguin with a worried frown.

"I'll see that they are delivered to your room at the palace," he assured her, glancing at his symbiot who sneezed and stood up.

"Oh, good," Sara replied with a relieved smile. "I've never had so many stuffed animals before. It's kind of fun collecting them."

"I am sure there will be many more," he promised with a chuckle.

He stood to the side so that Emma and Sara could step out of the room ahead of him. Sara felt another wave of warmth when he reached out a hand and ran it along her hip as she passed by him. She shot him a heated look, but he just looked at her with an innocent expression.

Innocent, my ass, she thought.

If he wasn't doing the little touches and hot looks, his dragon was! If she didn't know any better, she would think Jaguin and his dragon were working on a deliberate plan of attack on her senses. She had noticed an increase in their attention over the last week. A touch here, a look there, hot vivid images flashing through her mind, and that damn dragon purring every chance he got. It was slowly driving her and her body crazy – in a good way.

"Don't think I don't know what you and your dragon are doing! You even have Honey in on it. I want you to know you are not fighting fair," she muttered under her breath to him when he fell into step next to her.

"If it is working, why should I?" He retorted in a smooth voice that reminded her of rich, melted chocolate.

Sara's face heated when she saw him sniff the air and release a soft, almost inaudible growl. Another thing she had learned over the last couple of weeks: the Valdier had an extremely good sense of smell. Drawing in a deep breath, Sara cursed her body's reaction to him for the thousandth time. She was going to have to overcome her fears and self-doubt and just jump Jaguin's bones.

Then, maybe I'll get all of this craziness out of my system, she thought as they stepped out of the lift and into the deck lined with the various transports.

Chapter 13

Sara stared out the window of the rooms she and Emma had been given later that day. Her hand moved to her stomach and she absently rubbed it. This world was so different from Earth in so many ways, yet there were also similarities.

"If there is anything else you might need, just let me or one of the servants know," the woman with the long, dark hair said in a calm, soothing voice. "Morian has asked the seamstress to come by."

Sara turned and looked at Abby Tanner-Reykill. The tall, slender woman had come to visit shortly after their arrival. Her worried gaze had missed nothing and she had quickly taken Sara and Emma under her wing.

"Morian has prepared a dinner to welcome you tomorrow night," Abby was saying.

"Morian?" Sara asked in a husky tone.

Abby released a soft laugh. "It's a bit much remembering all the names. You won't have any trouble remembering Morian when you meet her. She is absolutely wonderful."

Sara nodded, turning back to look out over the gardens. She itched to get outside and explore all the plants that she had seen as Jaguin had led Sara and Emma through the gardens. Even Emma hadn't been immune to the beauty of the lush flowerbeds and unique designs combining water features with the unusual colors and textures of the flora.

Sara absently listened as Abby explained that Morian Reykill was Priestess to the Hive and the mother of the five Valdier Princes. The oldest, Zoran, was King of the Valdier and Abby's mate. She listened as Abby quietly told Sara about how she had found Zoran unconscious on her mountain outside Shelby, California. A deadly encounter with the sadistic sheriff had almost ended Abby's life.

"I know he would have killed me," Abby was saying in a voice that held a wealth of sadness. "He almost killed Carmen. If it hadn't been for Zoran and the others, she would have died. Clay had stabbed her. The technology and medical skills back on Earth are not as advanced as the Valdier."

"I know," Sara responded, thinking of her own dance with death. "I would have died, too."

"Oh, Sara. I'm so sorry," Abby whispered, coming to stand next to her.

Sara lifted a hand to brush it across her cheek, surprised when she felt that it was damp. She gave a derisive laugh and shook her head. Every time she thought she was getting a grip on her emotions, she found she was still carrying the damn baggage around. Deep down, she knew part of it was fear that she wouldn't see Jaguin again now that they were back on his planet.

"Maybe it would be for the best," she whispered.

"What would be for the best?" Abby asked.

Sara glanced at Abby and shook her head. "Nothing, just thinking aloud," she murmured, turning to look out over the garden again.

"Jaguin and Gunner have been assigned as your guards," Abby said after a few quiet seconds of silence. "They are both good men."

"I know," Sara replied, not looking at Abby.

She was afraid Abby would see the flare of relief in her eyes. Her fingers went instinctively to the band of gold on her arm when a wave of warmth filled her. For a split second, she felt Jaguin reach out and touch her. He had once told her that they were connected in a way that usually only happened after the Dragon's Fire. What that was, she wasn't sure, but she knew that it had something to do with a man and a woman coming together.

"Abby," Sara called out when Abby started to move away.

"Yes, Sara," Abby answered.

"What is the Dragon's Fire?" Sara asked suddenly, needing to know.

A rosy blush bathed Abby's cheeks and her eyes twinkled with warm light. Her lips curved upward and for a moment, Sara wasn't sure that she should have asked. It was obvious that Abby had to think about how to phrase her answer before she responded.

"The Dragon's Fire is an intense moment when a Valdier male claims his true mate," Abby explained, wrapping her arms around her waist. "It isn't painful as much as it is arousing. When the male bites the woman destined to be his mate, he breathes a part of his and his dragon's essence into her. I don't understand how it works, but it changes the woman."

"Into a dragon?" Sara asked in a husky voice.

Abby looked at her in surprise and nodded. "Yes, how did you know?" She asked.

Sara gave Abby a crooked smile. "I saw Melina change," she said, biting her lip. "Does... Does the male have to do that? When they make love... Does he have to bite me?"

Abby's expression softened. "I don't know," she said with a sympathetic smile. "I would think if he knew going in that you didn't want him to, he wouldn't, but Sara, if you are a warrior's true mate, it can be very dangerous if he does not claim you. His dragon... His dragon needs his mate much more than the man does."

Sara looked back at Abby. Her lips parted and she drew in a deep breath. Her gaze moved to her hands. She was twisting them together, which was another new habit she had developed since her captivity.

"What is it like to be a true mate to a Valdier warrior?" Sara asked in a soft voice, glancing up at Abby with a curious, worried gaze.

"It is the most wonderful feeling in the universe," Abby promised, stepping forward and cupping Sara's hands. "You have never known what it was like to be truly loved until you've found your other half." Abby lifted her right hand and cupped Sara's cheek gently, brushing a strand of hair back. "A warrior and his dragon will love you, protect you, and be there for you always."

Sara stared into Abby's eyes. "I've never had anyone but myself," she whispered.

"You do now," Abby promised.

Sara released a shaky breath when Abby wrapped her arms around her and held her tight. It was so strange to finally be with people who really cared about her as a person. For so long, she had been alone.

Never again, my elila, a husky voice whispered through her mind.

* * *

The next evening, Sara sat in the dining room. She fingered the beautiful gown that she was wearing. The last two days had flown by. Between visits with the seamstress, fittings, and settling in, she had barely had a chance to catch her breath!

Still, as busy as it had been, she'd still felt Jaguin's absence to her core. She had chided herself for her absurd feelings. She had never had a mental, much less a physical, craving to be around a man before. She actually *hurt* with a physical need to see Jaguin.

She had wanted to throw herself into Jaguin's arms when he had arrived earlier to escort Sara and Emma to the dining room, and she would have, if she hadn't been so busy making sure that Emma didn't disappear again into her bedroom.

"You look beautiful," Jaguin whispered, leaning closer to her.

Sara scowled and wiggled her nose. "I haven't worn a dress since I was ten," she muttered, fingering the material. "I feel... weird."

Jaguin's soft, husky chuckle washed over her. Sara pressed her legs together when she felt the familiar heat ignite between them. It was getting worse and worse. She glanced around the table, blushing when she saw several of the men at the table pause and turn in her direction.

"Stop it," she growled under her breath.

"And if I don't?" Jaguin teased, leaning forward so his warm breath fanned around her bare neck. "I want you, Sara."

Sara drew in a hissing breath. She knew her face was flushed, this time from desire, not embarrassment. Closing her eyes, she counted to ten before opening them again. She had to keep a grip on her emotions. Turning, she glanced at Emma. Her gaze swept over the other woman's face, noting that Emma's face was flushed as well.

"Are you alright?" Sara asked, leaning toward Emma. "You look flushed."

Sara noticed that Emma looked at her with huge, wary eyes before she leaned forward slightly to look pointedly at Jaguin. Sara glanced over her shoulder to see Jaguin was returning Emma's look.

"Does she have need of a healer?" Jaguin asked with a frown.

Sara shook her head. "No, I don't think so. Can't you go sit somewhere else?" She asked in exasperation.

Her body went from warm to an inferno when she felt his hand on her knee. He was not playing fair at all. She gritted her teeth when his hand slid further up her thigh. She swore if his hand went any higher, she would dump the glass of ice water sitting in front of her on his lap.

Jaguin gave her an amused look, as if he knew what she was thinking. "No," he replied with a sharp-toothed grin.

Sara couldn't quite contain the snort that escaped her. "Damn it all, Jaguin," she hissed under her breath. "You're driving me crazy."

Sara would have said more if she hadn't been so surprised when another male came to sit on the other side of Emma. Her eyes widened in alarm at the dark-haired man. There was an aura of barely suppressed savagery around him. For a moment, her mind was swept back to Columbia and her time with Cuello. She swayed in her seat, terror washing through her.

"What is your name, female?" The man's dark voice asked Emma. "I am called Ha'ven. You are too thin. You need to eat. You will eat, *misha petite*."

Sara pushed through her fear, her need to protect Emma overriding her own terror. Her gaze flew to her friend's face, sure that Emma would be petrified by the male. Instead, Sara was shocked to see Emma's eyes glittering with barely suppressed fury.

Sara blinked in confusion and returned her gaze to the man. "Leave her alone," she ordered, glaring at the man.

He shrugged off Sara's demand and returned his attention back to Emma. "She is too thin," Ha'ven replied, picking up a piece of fruit off of his plate. "If she does not wish me to feed her, she can tell me herself."

Sara stiffened, about to rise out of her seat when Jaguin leaned forward. His fingers tightened on her thigh, keeping her still. Sara sucked in a breath when Jaguin looked back at Ha'ven with a hint of warning in his gaze.

"Ha'ven, this one is not for you, my friend. She is not well," Jaguin insisted in a cool, calm voice.

Sara didn't know who was more surprised, herself, Emma, or the two men when Emma suddenly rose and excused herself. Sara started to rise, but Emma pressed her hand down against her shoulder and shook her head. Sara knew her mouth was hanging open when Emma shot the man named Ha'ven a heated look before turning on her heel and disappearing behind the nearby double doors.

"Well, that was strange," Sara whispered, turning in her seat to watch Emma, then Ha'ven, disappear through the doors.

"I think Ha'ven is in for a surprise," Jaguin murmured.

Sara turned to stare at him with a frown. "Why do you say that? Emma has to be terrified of him! He... He reminded me of Cuello," she added in a quiet, trembling voice. "I could feel the power rolling off of him."

Jaguin shook his head. "It was not fear in her eyes, Sara, it was fire. Ha'ven is the Curizan Prince. He is an honorable ally. He will not harm Emma," he assured her, glancing toward the doorway. A slight smile curved his lips. "If I had to bet, I would place my credits on Emma. Ha'ven is about to find out that he isn't as charming as he thinks he is."

Chapter 14

Jaguin watched as Sara talked quietly with the human doctor. They were comparing some of the places back on Earth that they had visited. His hand moved to touch her again when he saw her yawn.

"Would you like to see the gardens at night before you retire?" Jaguin asked in a husky voice.

Sara's eyes widened and the fatigue disappeared to be replaced with excitement and curiosity. She nodded and pushed back her chair with an apology to Audrey. Audrey smiled and shook her head.

"No problem," Audrey replied. "I'm still trying to settle in. I'm supposed to meet up with Tandor in the library. He was going to show me how to access some of the medical video logs."

Sara's eyes widened when Gunner grunted and muttered under his breath. She saw a troubled look flash through Audrey's eyes before they cleared. Leaning forward, she gave the other woman a hug.

"We've got to stick together," she whispered in Audrey's ear.

"Isn't that the truth!" Audrey responded with a sigh. "Enjoy your walk. I'm hoping Gunner will take me out to the gardens later. I'll need the break after stuffing my head full of facts."

Sara laughed and pulled away. "I'll be out in the garden stuffing my head full of facts," she replied with a grin. "Have fun."

Audrey nodded with a sigh, turning when Gunner stepped up to her. "Thanks."

Sara leaned into Jaguin when he rested his hand along her lower back. She could feel the warmth of it through the thin material of the gown. With a sigh, she felt the tension begin to fall away as they exited the dining room.

"Did I mention that the flowers are especially brilliant at night?" Jaguin asked as they turned and exited the dining room.

"No, but I saw some of them last night from the window of my room. I spent some time with Morian earlier today. She showed me her atrium. She has an amazing knowledge of the plants here. There are quite a few that I would like to study if I get a chance."

"Lady Morian's love for her gardens is well known. She designed all the ones you see here," Jaguin replied, threading her arm through his as they descended the steps.

Sara glanced up at Jaguin. "Will you turn into your dragon? How has he been doing? I missed him last night," Sara asked in concern when she felt the tautness of his muscles under her palm.

I tell you she like me more! His dragon growled.

Jaguin winced. He had felt the beast inside him moving restlessly throughout the dinner. His dragon had definitely missed Sara last night. Jaguin finally had to release him for a while. A smile curved his lips as a sudden thought came to him.

Yes! His dragon chuckled with glee. *Now? We do it now?*

Not yet, Jaguin replied in a calming voice. *Let me spend some time with her in the garden first. Then we'll show her the magic of our world.*

I bite? His dragon asked in a hopeful tone.

I hope so, Jaguin groaned. *I'm not sure I can hold out much longer.*

Me bite. She no get mad at me, his dragon retorted with confidence.

Yes, well, don't forget that you and I are one, Jaguin muttered. *I'll do the biting first and that is what she is going to remember.*

I make her happy. She no stay mad, his dragon promised.

Jaguin muttered under his breath. His dragon was going to get him in all kinds of trouble, and he had reached the point where he was going to let it. He needed Sara. It had gone beyond want. It was now a critical need. Just one day without her company and he had been half mad.

"What?" Sara asked, looking up at him as they turned the corner leading out to the large balcony.

"I said welcome to Valdier," Jaguin improvised, opening the door and waving his hand for her to go before him.

Liar, his dragon growled, practically prancing.

Just – shut up, Jaguin ordered, stepping out behind Sara.

* * *

Sara exclaimed again when another flower, this time with blue striped petals and a glowing filament and anther, opened up. Almost immediately, insects of varying sizes swarmed toward the light. Sara held her hand up so that she could compare the size of it to the flower.

"It's almost twice as big as my hand," she whispered, afraid to speak too loudly for fear of disturbing the magic of the moment. "This is incredible."

"There are plants near my village that are even larger," Jaguin replied. "Watch this."

Sara gasped when he knelt and ran his hand over another plant that provided a thick ground cover. The leaves lit up under his palm. Inside, Sara could see the vascular bundle pulse with dark green and bright yellow light. Sara stepped closer to examine it.

"Sara," Jaguin's soft groan pulled her attention to where she was standing.

Her face flushed when she realized that with him kneeling, her position put her breasts practically in his face. A sudden longing swept through her, searing her as if she were on fire. Her hands moved on their own, threading through his hair and holding him still as she bent forward and sealed her lips to his in a hot kiss filled with need and longing. She was tired of fighting the constant battle with her own desire. She wanted him.

His hands slid up her side, pulling the filmy material of the gown with it. A shiver went through her when the cool air touched her heated skin. If anything, it fanned the flames running through her.

"Jaguin, I need you," she murmured in a desperate whisper against his lips. "I want to make love with you. Will you stay with me tonight?"

Jaguin rose to his feet. His eyes glittered with the dark flames that she had grown accustomed to seeing in his eyes. The intense gaze promised her that he would grant her wish with relish.

"Do you trust me?" He asked in a husky tone.

Sara stared up at him and nodded. "Yes," she whispered.

"Then, be sure to hold on tight," he instructed, staring at her with a mysterious smile.

A confused frown creased Sara's brow for a moment before her eyes widened in understanding when he stepped back from her. Within seconds, Jaguin's dragon gazed back at her. Her head turned when she saw Honey suddenly appear. A portion of the symbiot flowed from Honey's large body. It wrapped around the dragon, forming a saddle and stirrups.

Sara's lips parted in amazement before her eyes shimmered with excitement. She stepped up to the dragon when he knelt down to her. Climbing onto the saddle, she wrapped her fingers around the grips.

Jaguin rose and turned his head to look at her. Sara reached out her left hand to caress his nostril. Once again, he had taken her by surprise.

"I'm ready," she whispered to the dragon.

The dragon bowed its head in agreement before turning. An excited laugh escaped Sara when she felt his muscles tighten before he pushed off the ground. His long wings swept back and forth in powerful strokes as they rose higher. From the air, Sara could see the edge of the garden and the cliff beyond.

She leaned forward when she felt Jaguin's body turn toward the vast ocean. From the corner of her eye, she caught a glimpse of the rest of Honey flying beside them. This time, Honey was in the shape of a large bird of prey.

Returning her attention to where they were going, she released a shriek of delight when Jaguin partially folded his wings inward as they swept over the short wall that ran around the garden. Sara held tightly onto the grip, laughing as they soared downward toward the waves crashing against the rocks far below.

Feeling her exhilaration, the symbiot flowed into thick bands of gold wrapping around her legs and body, steadying her, so that she could lift her arms upward. Sara gasped when Jaguin pulled up just above the waves. She could feel the dampness of the sea spray against her face. Her breath caught at the beauty of the water as the moon light sparkled off of it, making it appear alive.

"Oh, Jaguin," she breathed. "This is... This is unbelievable."

The dragon turned to look at her for a brief moment. Sara laughed when she saw his tongue hanging out of the side of his mouth. It was obvious he was enjoying this as well. She couldn't help but think it must be an incredible feeling to be able to fly like this.

As if reading her thoughts, Jaguin rose higher. His strong wings cut through the air. Sara could see where he was going. They went higher and higher, passing through several wispy clouds before they soared above them. There was nothing between them and the stars above or the ocean below.

For a moment, Sara was lost in the magic of the moment. Her heart slowed and she felt at peace. Releasing the grip again, she opened her arms wide and imagined that she was a dragon, flying upward to touch the stars.

You can be, if you wish, Jaguin's soft voice echoed in her mind.

Tears blinded Sara. Just the thought of such a possibility was enough to make her say yes. What would it be like to be so powerful, to never have to be afraid again?

To never be alone, she thought with a wave of longing.

Her gaze moved down to the diamond coated water. She noticed that they were heading inland. The dark shadows of massive trees below covered the landscape. They flew along a winding river, soaring upward when they reached a vast waterfall before continuing on.

Sara wasn't sure where Jaguin was taking her, but she wasn't worried. He continued along the river for several more miles before he turned once again. This time, he flew among the tall, thick trees. Moonlight shone through, giving Sara just enough light to see. Her lips parted again when he slowed and landed on a massive branch several meters above the ground.

The silver dragon walked with confidence along the branch. It wasn't until they were closer to the trunk that Sara saw a rough-cut platform nestled between the fork of three branches.

Once they were on it, the gold holding Sara secure in her seat dissolved, freeing her. Sara carefully slid off of Jaguin's back, jumping slightly when his tail wound around her waist to steady her.

"I'm okay," she whispered, stroking the silky scales. "Where are we?" She asked, turning in a circle.

"I like to come here when I need time alone," Jaguin murmured. "It is too far to return to my village when I am needed at the palace. I have quarters there, but there are times when I crave the solitude of the forest."

Sara turned, startled to hear Jaguin's husky, deep voice. Her arms reached out and her hands gripped his shoulders when he wrapped his arms around her waist. They stood like that for a moment, neither moving. As if in slow motion, Sara rose up on her toes and tilted her head.

Jaguin's soft moan echoed around them before she captured it with her lips. Her fingers splayed in his hair. She enjoyed its silky texture as she deepened the kiss. Her lips parted and she touched his lips with her tongue. The moment he opened his mouth, her tongue swept inside in a kiss that promised a night they would never forget.

Chapter 15

Jaguin felt a burst of pleasure as their heated breaths mixed. A soft groan escaped him when Sara's fingers tightened in his hair and she leaned into him. Her mumbled words sank in at the same time as her lips ran along his jaw.

"I need you, Jaguin," she murmured.

"Sara," Jaguin groaned again when he felt her fingers tracing down his skin.

"You've been driving me crazy," she muttered, sliding her hands down his neck to his shoulders before moving them to the front of his shirt. "Tell me that you want this as much as I do," she pleaded as she worked the fastenings of his shirt.

A strangled sound escaped Jaguin. "You have no idea," he muttered.

Sara's soft laughter filled the air, surrounding him in its warmth. Jaguin's eyes closed as she slowly pulled his shirt out of his waistband and pushed the material off his shoulders. His throat worked up and down when she leaned forward and brushed her lips along his heated skin.

"I've dreamed of doing this," she whispered, pressing small kisses across his flesh. "There is something about you that makes me want to taste every inch of you."

Jaguin's jaw tightened and he opened his eyes to stare up at the one visible moon that lit the sky. A shudder ran through him when Sara teased one of his nipples with her teeth. The image of her lips pressed against his body sent a powerful shaft of need through him, filling his cock. He was painfully aware of his need for her.

I bite, his dragon hissed, moving deep inside him.

Not yet, Jaguin growled in return.

My mate. I want my mate, his dragon demanded, straining against his control.

"So beautiful," Sara whispered, caressing the scales rippling over his skin. "I can see your dragon in your eyes."

Both Jaguin and his dragon stilled at her hushed words, listening in fascination. He slowly lowered his gaze to watch her.

"There's a fire in your eyes. I was afraid the first time I saw it. The flames danced as if they had a life of their own," she continued, stroking his skin as she moved around him. Her hands touched his arms, his shoulders, and his back before sliding down to his hips. Her lips drew a line of fire across his back, from shoulder blade to shoulder blade. "It took me a little while to figure out that it was your dragon. I see those flames in his eyes whenever you shift forms. I don't understand how you can be so different, but you are."

"Sara," Jaguin murmured in a husky voice when her hands moved to the front fastenings of his trousers. "You are playing with fire. I barely have control of my dragon. He wishes to complete the mating between us. Tonight... tonight you will be ours."

Sara's fingers paused on the top fastening for a brief second. Jaguin could feel the tremble in them. He bowed his head, waiting to see if she would continue. He would not force her. If she decided that this was not what she wanted, he would have to have his symbiot return her to the palace. Deep down, he knew he was not strong enough to do so.

A soft hiss escaped him when her fingers unhooked the first fastening before moving to the second, then the third one. He turned when she was finished and bent to unfasten the strap holding his boots on. He slid one then the other off, before he straightened. The movement caused his trousers to slide lower on his hips.

His hands instinctively moved upward to the catch on Sara's dress when she turned her back to him. Brushing her hair to the side, he carefully undid the fastening and slid it down. Her creamy skin was slowly revealed as he pulled it down to the top of her buttocks. Leaning forward, he pressed his lips against the heated flesh of her shoulder.

Her hands dropped to her side when he tenderly pushed the silky material down. It fell in a soft, light blue wave around her ankles. Under the dress she wore nothing more than a thin covering of lace over her buttocks.

"I've never been very big up top," she whispered, guiding his hands around to cup the small mounds. "It has its advantages."

Her voice broke when he cupped her breasts in his large, warm palms. A soft cry of need escaped her when his forefinger and thumb captured the taut peaks. Her hips moved backwards against him and he could smell the delicious scent of her arousal in the night air.

His fingers tightened on her hips when she leaned back and tilted her head. Jaguin's lips pressed against the soft skin of her shoulder. He could feel the intense heat building inside him as the Dragon's Fire rose up. A soft groan escaped him when Sara rubbed back against him. It was the blade that sliced through the fragile hold he had on his dragon. With a whispered plea for forgiveness, he turned his face into her neck and pierced the tender flesh over her pulse.

Sara's loud cry filled the air. She didn't pull away from him as he thought she might. Instead, she clutched his hands to her breasts and held still as he breathed the Dragon's Fire into her. Pulling his right hand free, he slid it down over her stomach. His fingers moved under the lacy fabric of her panties to thread through the soft covering of hair.

"Yes!" Sara's softly groaned plea caressed him.

He felt her hips rock back and forth as he continued to breath the fire into her. His dragon roared in triumph. Tonight, his mate would be born. Jaguin had no doubt that Sara was strong enough to survive the Dragon's Fire. She was the strongest female he had ever known.

He clutched her to him when she began to move more urgently against him. He could feel the fire coursing through her veins. His own body rippled with the colors of his dragon in response. His cock strained against the covering of his trousers. He could feel Sara's heat through the course material.

Sara's body melted back against his as the Dragon Fire took hold of her. Sliding his fingers down, he savored the dampness of her arousal that pooled between her legs. She moved back and forth against his fingers at an increasingly frantic pace. He released his grip on her neck and ran his tongue over the mark that was beginning to form at the same time as she came in his arms.

"Yes!" She moaned in a long, breathless hiss. "Oh, Jaguin, yes!"

"Now, Sara," Jaguin muttered in a guttural tone.

He felt Sara sway in his arms as she turned. He gripped her hips, his fingers snapping the fragile material covering her on each side. Her hands were moving desperately to his hips and she pushed his trousers down. Jaguin released a strangled curse when she wrapped her hand around his throbbing cock.

"Form a bed now," he ordered his symbiot.

Honey transformed in seconds. Jaguin reached down and covered Sara's hand. His eyes glittered with a fiery passion.

"I want to do this right," he gritted out.

Sara shook her head and pulled him back toward the golden bed. "You already have," she whispered back to him. "Jaguin!" She suddenly gasped as a fierce wave of heat rose up inside her.

"It is the Dragon's Fire," Jaguin murmured, lifting a hand to brush against her cheek. "Tonight I claim you, Sara. In every way a warrior can – as my true mate."

"I was already on fire for you," she breathed, gripping his shoulders and turning them both so she could push him down on the bed. "To hell with doing this the right way. There is no wrong way between us."

Jaguin was about to protest when Sara slid down between his legs. Her hand wrapped around his cock again, this time in a firm grip. His lips parted when she leaned forward and wrapped her lips around the tip. His eyes widened and his breath exploded outward when she continued to slide her lips down.

His hips jerked upwards and a strangled cry escaped him when she began moving up and down. He had never experienced anything like this before. His head would have fallen back in ecstasy if not for the fact that he couldn't look away from the beautiful sight of her lips around him.

"Sara," he whispered when she looked up at him. "Oh, yes!"

* * *

Sara savored the feel of power coursing through her. The fire was building; and instead of fighting it, she embraced it. She wanted Jaguin in a way she had never wanted any other man.

Her lips caressed his cock while her hand moved up and down along the smooth, hard shaft. She poured her love into her touch. She wanted him to feel what she could not say in words – that she loved him with every fiber of her being.

She allowed her other hand to caress his heavy sack, rolling it gently against her palm. His loud moan and the way his legs fell apart told her that he was enjoying her touch. Her gaze rose and locked on his again. She could see the gold in Jaguin's eyes and the burning liquid flames of his dragon.

A fierce shaft of painful need struck her again, but Sara relished the intense feeling. She controlled it, not allowing the discomfort of her own need to take away from what she was doing. She was claiming Jaguin – one stroke, one kiss at a time.

Pulling back, she stared at Jaguin. "You are so powerful," she whispered. "I love the feel of you."

"Sara...," Jaguin started to say before his voice died and he groaned.

Sara's moan mixed with Jaguin's as she bent her head again. The fire poured through her with so much intensity that she thought she was going to have an orgasm without any other stimulation, a definite first for her. Releasing his cock, she slowly began working her way up his body. Her lips paused on a faint scar. It was low on his right hip. She knew from talking to Tandor that only scars from grievous injuries were impossible to completely erase. Tandor had explained it to her so she could understand why he could not erase all of the scars that crisscrossed her back.

Pain at the thought of how close he had come to dying before she ever had a chance to meet him hit her hard. Sara pressed a kiss to the scar before tracing it with her tongue. Jaguin's hips rocked, encouraging her to continue her explorations.

"I swear you will be the death of me, Sara," Jaguin ground out as she slowly climbed up his body. "I need you now!"

Sara's lips parted in a gasp when Jaguin suddenly sat up and gripped her under her arms. She felt her body being lifted as if she was no heavier than a child before he settled her over his hips. His cock strained upward, throbbing against her saturated core. His eyes glowed with dark flames.

She leaned forward, balanced by her hands and knees. She held up one hand, daring him to remain still as she reached down between them to grasp his throbbing cock once again.

"I claim you, Jaguin," Sara whispered, waiting as the fire inside her built to a crescendo of desire and need. The moment it crested, she sank down on him, impaling herself as far as she could go. "Jaguin!"

Her loud cry reverberated through the forest, sending the night birds flying. Sara's head fell back and a loud sob escaped her at the feeling of fullness stretching her, filling every empty void inside her with Jaguin's essence. Her fingers kneaded his chest as he gripped her hips and began moving in a hard, steady rhythm that increased as her slick moisture coated his cock.

Jaguin's soft words washed over her as he moved. She groaned, feeling every inch of him as he pushed deeper and deeper until she swore they were no longer two separate entities, but one. His fingers dug into her hips, holding her as he rocked with one powerful thrust after another.

"You are mine, Sara. I claim you as my true mate. No others may have you. I will live to protect you. You are my mine – forever, *elila*. My true mate, my gift from the goddess," Jaguin bit out, straining upward as the last words escaped his lips and his body exploded inside her.

Sara felt her body respond to his claim. Bending forward, she repeated his words in a broken whisper, her body igniting in wave after wave the faster he moved.

"You… are… mine, Jaguin," Sara gasped, sliding her hands over his shoulders. "I claim you… as… as… my… true mate. No… others… may have you. I will live to protect you. You are mine… forever. Oh, Jaguin, help me!"

"Now, Sara! Give in to the change. Let it take you, my brave, beautiful mate. Let it take you," Jaguin encouraged, holding her tight as he pulsed inside her.

"Ahhhh!" Sara cried out, turning her face into his neck and biting him to keep from screaming.

"Dragon's balls!" Jaguin groaned as his body reacted to her orgasm.

* * *

Nothing had prepared Jaguin for the intensity of the Dragon's Fire. He'd had sex with plenty of women over the centuries, but nothing like this. This wasn't sex. This wasn't just a fleeting encounter to relieve his sexual needs. This was a connection of two souls becoming one. His eyes widened when he saw a ripple of scales move over Sara's skin.

A combination of feelings rushed through Jaguin. He was witnessing the birth of his dragon's mate. Dark ash and silver scales, slightly darker than his own, moved across Sara's chest, arms, and up along her throat. His fingers tightened on her hips.

Jaguin swore nothing in his life could compare to watching the birth of Sara's dragon. He could feel the changes as if they were his own. He raised one shaky hand to touch a line of the scales before they disappeared. His breath caught when Sara suddenly slid forward and pressed her breasts against him. He could feel the sweat beading on her body.

A low groan escaped him when he felt her slick walls pulsing as he continued to push in and out of her. The feel of his cock sliding against her heated core and the way both were swelling to lock together was enough to drive him mad. He felt the wave of fire building inside her again. He waited until it reached its peak before he pushed up and spilled his seed into her.

Shock ricocheted through him when she turned her head into his neck and bit down. His body strained upward at the sudden mixture of pleasure and pain. He strained, his muscles taut as he pulsed deep inside her in a mating that sealed the ancient bond between true mates – both as a man and a woman and as dragons.

"Dragon's balls!" Jaguin groaned and shuddered. He lay there a moment, breathing hard.

Night just start! His dragon crowed in delight. *Again! I want mate. Again! Again!*

Between you and Sara, you two are going to kill me, Jaguin gasped as another shudder ran through him when he felt the fire reignite. *Wait...*

No wait! Again! His dragon roared, breathing the fire inside Jaguin to life again.

Dragon's balls! Jaguin's shuddering groan escaped him when he felt his cock come to life once more.

Yes! Good balls. Dragons have big ones, his dragon urged.

"I know dragons have big balls," Jaguin retorted in an exasperated tone.

"TMI, Jaguin," Sara softly giggled when he unknowingly responded to his dragon's comment out loud.

"Again," Jaguin muttered, rolling so that he was on top this time. "The night has just begun."

Sara's eyes widened and her face flushed when Jaguin ground his hips against her and reached up to pinch her nipples. Her lips parted on another cry when his hands moved down to hold her thighs so he could begin riding her again. His eyes fastened on her neck and the faint mark of the dragon on it. Before the night was over, his mark would be on several different parts of her body. He and his dragon would make sure of that.

Chapter 16

Sara snuggled against Jaguin. His arm was wrapped tightly around her. The faint colors of early dawn were beginning to streak the sky. The memories of the night replayed in her mind over and over. The Dragon's Fire had burned throughout the night with such intensity that Sara was surprised the flames hadn't consumed her and Jaguin.

A small smile curved her lips as she thought back to yesterday afternoon after Abby had left. She had spent a good portion of the day thinking about what she had to return to if she went back to Earth. The answer had been the same no matter which way she tried to approach it. There was nothing; no family who cared about her, no job, nothing. Her job at the university had been funded by a grant that would have already run out of money by the time she returned, which would leave her scrambling to find another post. There was nothing for her there, except bad memories and loneliness.

She turned her head and gazed at Jaguin's peaceful face. She hadn't lied when she'd told him that she was already on fire. Her feelings for him were different from anything she had ever experienced before. He made her want things that she had never even thought about. For the first time in her life, she wanted a place to call home, possibly even a family. The plants here were unusual and fascinating. She could spend a lifetime learning about them and still never understand it all.

All through dinner, her heart had pounded with nervousness. If that hadn't been enough, a small measure of self-doubt about whether or not she was making the right decision had plagued her as well. Those doubts had dissolved the moment he had guided her out of the dining room and they had stepped out into the garden.

The tender look in Jaguin's eyes when he'd reached down to show her the ground cover had melted her heart. She wanted him – all of him. Their journey to the forest had sealed her decision.

Sara blinked in surprise when she felt Jaguin's fingers along her cheek. Tilting her head back to gaze at him, she saw that he was staring back at her with an assessing gaze. She gave him a tentative smile, unsure of what to do.

"You look deep in thought," he commented.

"Not really," Sara murmured, looking back to the sky. "I've always loved the early mornings. The colors, the freshness as the world wakes up."

"Sara, I will not leave you," Jaguin said, lifting her hand to his lips. "I can feel your fear."

Sara stiffened for a moment before she sat up. A low rumble escaped Jaguin when the silky cover of the symbiot pooled around her lap. She turned and raised her eyebrow at Jaguin.

"I thought we finally extinguished the fire," she laughed.

Jaguin sat up and wrapped his arms around her. "Never!" He swore, burying his face in the curve of her shoulder. "We could always greet the day."

Sara laughed again and scooted off the bed, taking the thin covering with her. She shivered when it moved over her body. For a moment, she had forgotten that the blanket was actually alive. Dropping it, she bent and picked up her dress.

"Stop it," she playfully growled when she felt Jaguin press against her. "I need to visit the ladies room. Since I doubt that there is one here, I need to visit a tree. I also need a shower."

Jaguin sighed and reached for his own clothing. Sara paused, her eyes glued to his body as he pulled on the black trousers he had worn last night. She started when he chuckled and tipped her head back to press a hard kiss to her lips.

"You are not making this easy for me," he replied in a husky tone.

"Jaguin…," Sara whispered, staring into his eyes.

Jaguin's gaze softened when he saw the confusion in her gaze. Sara knew he could feel her uncertainty and that made her feel even more vulnerable. She closed her eyes and tilted her cheek into his palm when he slid his hand up to cup it.

"Everything will be well, Sara," Jaguin promised.

Sara didn't reply. Instead, she nodded and stepped back to finish getting dressed. Things always appeared different in the daylight – more exposed. Right now, she just needed time. Last night had been wonderful, but it had also taken by her surprise.

Abby had warned her that the Dragon's Fire would be intense. It wasn't the lovemaking that had stunned her. No, she had thoroughly enjoyed that, finding a sense of fulfillment that she had never experienced before. What had shocked her were the ash-colored scales that had danced along her skin. Her mind immediately went to Melina.

Was it really possible? Could she and Jaguin's coming together have changed her on a molecular level? It seemed impossible, even though she had witnessed the evidence herself.

"How do we get down?" Sara asked, walking over to the edge of the platform and glancing over the side. "Wow! I didn't realize we were so far up!"

"My symbiot will take us," Jaguin said as he finished fastening his shirt.

Sara glanced over to where Honey had been, but the bed and blanket were gone. She frowned, glancing around. Her eyes widened when she saw Honey in the shape of a mid-sized transport. A bridge between the seats and the platform suddenly formed.

Jaguin held his hand out to Sara. "After you," he said with a smile.

Sara shook her head and laughed. "I swear I've fallen through the looking glass," she said, reaching out to hold his hand as she stepped onto the bridge.

A short time later, they were speeding through the forest again. Sara laughed when Honey sped up along the riverbed. Her hair whipped wildly behind her.

Lifting her face to the early morning sunlight, she focused on the beauty of the morning and not the shadows that stood waiting on the edge of her consciousness.

* * *

Jaguin frowned when he saw Mandra Reykill standing on the balcony when they arrived back at the palace. Mandra had his arms crossed and was staring moodily out over the garden area. He looked up at their approach.

"Jaguin," Mandra greeted, glancing at Sara and giving her a brief nod of acknowledgement.

"What is wrong?" Jaguin asked with a dark frown.

Mandra glanced at Sara, his gaze pausing on the mark on her neck. A shimmer of amusement crossed his face and he reached out to slap Jaguin on the arm. Jaguin's own expression relaxed when he saw the smile on his friend's face.

"It is good to see you have claimed your true mate. Creon told me about your difficulty controlling your dragon. Has it had a chance to take his mate yet?" Mandra asked with a curious look at Sara.

Sara's eyes flashed. "That is none of your damn business," she snapped.

"No, it isn't," a feminine voice behind the huge male stated dryly.

Jaguin couldn't quite hide the grin when Mandra grimaced. He tilted his head to the side to look at the woman coming down the steps. Jaguin's gaze flickered back to Mandra when he slowly turned and gave the woman a huge smile.

"Hello, Ariel," Jaguin greeted.

"Hi, Jaguin," Ariel responded with a grin. She stopped next to Mandra and threaded her arm through the other warrior's bent arm. Turning her attention to Sara, she gave a warm smile. "Hi, I'm Ariel."

Sara's eyes widened. She gave Ariel a tentative smile. Her gaze moved back and forth between the slender woman and the huge male next to her.

"Hi," Sara replied, self-consciously fingering the material of her gown. "If you'll excuse me, I need to return to my room. I'll see you later."

"Sara," Jaguin started to say.

He paused when Mandra stepped forward and touched his arm. Irritation flashed through him before he concealed it. He knew that Mandra would not have stopped him if it wasn't important.

"There is a meeting," Mandra said. "We need you there."

Jaguin glanced back to where Sara had vanished through the doorway. Ariel quietly excused herself. Jaguin suspected Mandra's mate knew of his concern for leaving Sara so soon after their mating.

"She has not shifted yet," Jaguin finally said, turning to stare at Mandra.

"Our mate will stay with Sara and the other female," Mandra assured him. "Come."

Jaguin nodded, glancing once more toward the doors before he turned away. "What has happened?"

Chapter 17

Sara turned away from the window when she heard a knock on the door to her and Emma's living quarters. She brushed her hand over Honey's silky head for reassurance. The symbiot had not left her side since she had stepped out of the shower.

Drawing in a deep breath, Sara thought about everything that had happened since she, Jaguin, and Honey returned earlier. It had been almost six hours since they had returned to the palace. She had quickly showered and changed into jeans and a soft pink T-shirt. It felt good to be back in something that she felt more comfortable wearing.

Abby and the woman she'd met earlier, Ariel, had come by shortly after she had cleaned up to say that she and Emma would have to remain in their suite of rooms for a few days.

"Unfortunately, even this world has its problems," Abby had explained.

"Yeah, a bad-ass S.O.B. that needs his balls roasted over an open fire, preferably while they are still attached," Ariel had retorted.

"I'm afraid I have to agree with Ariel this time," Abby had replied quietly.

Sara had listened as Abby and Ariel explained what was going on. It appeared that there were evil men in every world, even alien ones. Shortly afterward, Abby and Ariel had excused themselves.

Sara, exhausted from the night before, had decided she would try to rest.

She should have known better. Even as exhausted as she was, the nightmares still came. Fearful of distracting Jaguin, she had forced herself back to consciousness and risen.

She jerked when she heard the sound of a knock again. A quick glance showed her that Emma had disappeared into her rooms again. Between stress of her nightmares and her worry for Emma, Sara felt like she was walking a tightrope that was beginning to fray in the storm.

Sara walked over to the door and opened it. Her gaze immediately froze on Jaguin. His hair was pulled back, but she could see that it was slightly wet. She gripped the door when her body swayed toward his.

"Hi," Sara whispered, staring up at him.

"You look tired," Jaguin said, reaching out to touch her cheek. "I felt your withdrawal earlier."

"I'm fine," she said, biting her lip.

Sara glanced at Gunner, who was standing back, trying to look at everything but them. She took a step back and motioned for them to come into the room. Jaguin stepped through, followed by Gunner.

"Where's Audrey?" Sara asked when Gunner stepped by her.

A flash of pain darkened Gunner's eyes before he shrugged. He continued into the room before he glanced at her again. She could see the same teasing smile on his lips that he normally wore when she saw him.

"She is with Tandor going over some medical information," Gunner replied. "She will be here shortly. Where is the other female?"

Sara wrapped her arms around her waist for a moment before she dropped them when she saw Jaguin frown. She could see the worry in his eyes. She gave him a tight smile and shook her head, glancing briefly at Gunner before she returned his gaze.

"Emma is in her room. She isn't comfortable being around others," Sara explained.

"That is not good for her," Gunner said with a frown. "She must learn to accept her new life."

Sara stiffened and glared at Gunner. "What would you know about what it is like to have to accept a new life?" She asked heatedly as she took a step toward him. "What do you know about being ripped from everything you've ever known and taken to not only a new life, but an alien world when you didn't even know aliens existed? How would you feel if you had to leave everything and everyone you knew and loved behind?"

Gunner frowned. "Why would you want to remain on a world where you were tortured by the men?" He asked.

"Gunner!" Jaguin's sharp tone mixed with Audrey's.

Sara stumbled backwards and paled. She clenched her trembling fingers to conceal her distress and shook her head at Jaguin when he took a step toward her. Sara turned away and walked stiffly over to the window, shutting the two men out.

"Sara..." Jaguin began in a gentle, comforting tone, unsure of what to say. Sara ignored him.

"Let me talk to her," Audrey said to Jaguin, closing the door behind her. "You talk to Warrior Man."

"Warrior Man? I attacked Tandor once! Just once!" Gunner muttered with a groan, running a hand through his hair. "I swear that female has more names for me than my own mother did when I was growing up."

Sara could feel Jaguin's concerned gaze on her. As much as she wanted to open her heart and mind to him, she felt too frazzled to handle it right now.

"Where's Emma?" Audrey asked in a quiet voice, walking up to stand next to her.

"Emma doesn't like it when others are around," Sara replied in a quiet tone. "Those are the two that brought us aboard the warship. They were there when we..." Sara's voice broke.

"I remember," Audrey replied in a gentle tone. "You're exhausted, Sara. Are you still not sleeping?"

Sara shook her head. "I'm sorry, Audrey. I'm so exhausted that I just can't think straight. I'd hoped after...." Her voice faded and she glanced over to where Jaguin and Gunner were quietly talking. "I'd hoped things wouldn't be so bad. I really wanted to start over, but every time I close my eyes...." Sara turned to look at Audrey. "Will it ever get better? I'm not the only one having trouble, so is Emma. I'm worried about her. She seems even more withdrawn than ever."

"It will take time, for both of you. What you went through isn't something that you can just shut off," Audrey said soothingly. "I worry that Emma isn't showing any improvement, though. I hoped that she would have begun to show some progress by now."

"It's hard," Sara whispered, tears burning her eyes. "I never used to be afraid. Now... Now, I don't like being around other... people. I can understand where Emma is coming from." Sara bowed her head.

Audrey touched Sara's arm. "Sara, you and Emma have been through a very traumatic experience. I would be surprised if you weren't both suffering from some form of PTSD. There is nothing to be ashamed of," Audrey assured her.

"What is PTSD?" Jaguin demanded, stepping closer. His gaze was glued to Sara's face. "You said you were fine. I thought my symbiot healed your wounds. Your head is not hurting again, is it?"

"Do you mind?" Sara hissed in aggravation, embarrassed that he had overheard their conversation when she was trying to spare him her emotional baggage. "I was having a private conversation and you were not invited to participate!"

Sara felt a wave of frustration when Jaguin ignored her and turned to glare at Audrey. "Do you know how to heal this PTSD?" He demanded.

"This is a private conversation between myself and Sara, but I will explain what PTSD is. It stands for Post-Traumatic Stress Disorder. It often occurs after an individual has suffered a terrifying ordeal, often from physical harm or the threat of physical harm. What Emma and Sara went through would definitely classify as such an ordeal," Audrey said in a cool, calm tone.

"Audrey, I don't want to talk about it. Especially with him here," Sara whispered in a strained voice filled with exhaustion, glancing toward Gunner, who stood watching them.

"I was there, Sara," Jaguin said tightly, not realizing that she wasn't looking at him, but at Gunner. "I saw what was done to you."

Sara's eyes darkened and for a moment it was as if her exhausted mind took her back to the damp prison cell in the jungles of Columbia. The world around her melted for that fraction of a second and she could once again hear Cuello's chilling laughter as he order his henchman to whip her.

A low, guttural cry escaped her and Sara stumbled backwards, shaking her head. She felt as if she were suffocating when Jaguin's distressed face came back into view. This time she knew that she had not been successful in keeping the images to herself. Sara's body shook and she shook her head when he took a step toward her. Afraid of her inability to control the horrible memories, Sara turned and bolted for her room.

"Sara!" Jaguin called after her. "Don't!"

"Enough!" Audrey ordered, stepping between him and Sara's fleeing form. She placed her hand on Jaguin's chest and shook her head. "I'll go to her. You two… just stay here and make sure no one takes the silverware."

* * *

Jaguin watched as Audrey followed Sara. He knew the human doctor did not understand that he knew more than she did about the nightmares that Sara was having, yet something told him that she might be able to help Sara in a way he could not. He turned when he felt a hand on his shoulder.

"Give her time. You were there. You know what was done to her." Gunner murmured.

"But not everything," Jaguin replied in a quiet voice. "I don't know everything that was done to her. She has shown me small fragments of what happened to her, Gunner, but there is more. I could help her if she would let me. Why can she not trust me to protect her? She is ashamed of her fears, but she shouldn't be. If I knew what happened, I could take the burden from her mind."

"You may never know," Gunner replied in a quiet, sympathetic tone. "Just accept and support her. That is all you can do."

"I will be there for her, even if she refuses to accept me," Jaguin whispered, turning to look dejectedly at his friend. "I thought last night would have shown her how I feel about her."

Gunner suddenly grinned and slapped Jaguin on the shoulder. "Since when have you ever accepted defeat?" He demanded with a raised eyebrow. "You have a challenge, my friend, to get her to accept you. Now, you must think of the best way to break down her barriers. You made a good start last night if the mark on her neck is anything to go by. Perhaps if you wake her dragon, she will realize that she has the power to destroy the demons that chase her. It worked for Carmen. Creon said she turned the human male who killed her first mate to ash. Perhaps that is what your Sara needs to do."

Jaguin's eyes narrowed and he thought for a moment before a slow smile curved his lips. "You are right, Gunner. I think it is time I took this challenge to more familiar ground. Somewhere I know and somewhere that she won't be able to resist going," he murmured, rubbing his chin as he stared down the hall where Sara had disappeared.

"How do you plan to do that? I might need to steal your idea," Gunner quickly added when Jaguin cast him a quick, assessing look.

"She loves unusual plants. I know a place where there are all kinds of unusual ones," Jaguin said thoughtfully as a plan began to form in his mind. "After things are taken care of here, I will return with her to my home in the Eastern Mountains. I think it is time that Sara met my family. I will also show her the house I have been working on. Together, we will make it into a home."

"You are too cunning for your own good sometimes. Now, what do you think my mate meant when she told us to make sure no one took the silverware?" Gunner asked, mirroring Jaguin by rubbing his jaw as he stared down the hallway for an entirely different reason.

* * *

Sara sat in the chair near the window, gazing out. She could feel the tension in the air. It was more than what had just happened, something else was going on. She could only think it had to do with the situation that Abby and Ariel had told her a little bit about earlier.

Reaching down, she absently stroked Honey's head that was resting on her lap. Gentle waves of warmth flowed through her. She sniffed and bowed her head. She was so tired.

"What is wrong with me?" She whispered.

You... need... me, a soft voice whispered in her head.

Sara froze, a frown creasing her brow. Slowly lifting her head, she looked around the room. That voice was... different.

"Now I'm going mad," Sara whispered in despair, closing her eyes.

No mad, just sad, the voice answered, this time a little stronger.

Who... Who are you? Sara asked silently.

You... but, me, the voice said.

"That makes absolutely no sense," Sara muttered out loud.

"What makes no sense, Sara?" Audrey asked, quietly closing the door behind her.

Sara started. She was amazed at how quiet Audrey was. This was the second time that she had entered a room without Sara being aware of it. Sara couldn't help but wonder if doctors took a class in how to walk stealthily.

A rumbling giggle in her mind shook her. Sara rose from her seat and swiveled in a tight circle, confused. Her hand rose to her head as a wave of dizziness struck her.

"Is your head hurting you again?" Audrey asked in concern.

"No… No, it's… I hear a voice in my head," Sara reluctantly admitted, suddenly afraid she had really lost her grip on reality.

Audrey moved forward and motioned for Sara to sit back down. She quickly checked both of Sara's eyes and pulse. Sara was surprised when she pulled a small scanner similar to what Tandor used out of the pocket of her long skirt. Sara sat still while Audrey scanned her. The other woman frowned down at the readings before she pulled the chair across from Sara closer and sat down.

"Your pulse is a bit fast, but I think it is okay considering your current emotion and physical state. The rest of the scan appears normal…," Audrey stated, glancing down at the readings with another frown.

Sara rubbed her damp palms along the material of her jeans. "You don't sound very convinced," she observed, glancing at the scanner in curiosity.

"The readings all say normal, but they are different than before," Audrey admitted.

That because I not there before, the voice in her head said.

Sara started again and stared at Audrey in growing panic. "There it is again," she exclaimed in a tight voice. "I just heard the voice again."

Audrey frowned and stared at Sara. "What did it say?" She asked.

"That the readings were different because she wasn't there before," Sara repeated in a voice that trembled.

Audrey leaned forward and gently held Sara's hair away from her neck. The frown slowly melted when she saw the mark on Sara's neck. Sara watched as Audrey sat back in her seat with a reassuring smile on her lips.

"You've mated with Jaguin, haven't you?" Audrey asked.

A blush rose, coloring Sara's cheeks a rosy color. "Yes, last night…," she mumbled.

"Can you ask the voice in your head if she is a dragon?" Audrey asked with a soothing smile.

"A dragon?!" Sara's stunned whisper echoed through the room.

My mate need me, the voice whispered. *You need me. You… you are a dragon?* Sara asked, stunned.

I your dragon, the voice replied. *You let me out. I show you.*

I don't know how, Sara replied in a small voice.

Our mate teach us, her dragon said confidently. *You see.*

What… What happens to me when… if I let you out? Sara asked.

We one. You still there, only inside, her dragon whispered. *I tired. You not sleep. I need sleep. You need sleep.*

"Sara," Audrey called several times before Sara heard her.

"Wh… What?" Sara asked, dazed.

Audrey leaned forward and cupped her hands. "I asked what did the voice say?"

"She said… She said she was tired. That I'm not sleeping and that we both need sleep," Sara admitted, blinking several times to clear her vision.

"She's right. Are the nightmares still as bad as they were before?" Audrey asked in a gentle tone, reaching into her pocket and pulling a small black bag the size of a clutch purse out.

"They change. Some are worse than others," Sara said, pulling her hair back. "Just when I think I have everything under control, they start up again. It's the unpredictability of them that keeps me feeling off-balance. It's like I never know what is going to trigger them. I feel like an emotional basket case…."

Audrey reached over and squeezed her hand. "It is totally understandable to be feeling like this, Sara. What you've been through has been very traumatic. Each person handles the stress in a different way. Don't be ashamed of your feelings. If you need to be alone, be alone, but don't give up. Talking about it helps some people. Other people find a hobby or a change of environment helps. Mediation, eating properly, and a daily routine will help you. Is there anything that you really love to do that you can do here?"

Sara drew in a deep breath and nodded. "I loved my job," she confessed, turning to look back out at the garden. "There are so many different plants here. It is amazing. I could spend the rest of my life just studying the ones in the garden."

"Then focus on that. Do what you love and don't worry about anything else," Audrey encouraged. "I'm going to give you something to help you get some rest."

Sara nodded, willing to do anything at the moment to just shut down for a little while. Her gaze moved to the door. For a brief second, she wished that Jaguin would hold her like he had on the ship, but she realized that now was not the time. He and Gunner were there to protect them from whatever was going on elsewhere in the palace. Drawing in a deep breath, she smiled at Audrey and lifted her arm to her.

Sara waited as Audrey withdrew a small vial and an injector from the bag she had pulled out a few minutes before. Sara watched in silence as Audrey inserted the vial into the injector before she pressed it against the inside of Sara's arm. Almost immediately, Sara felt the effects of the powerful drug.

A sigh of relief escaped Sara when Audrey slipped an arm around her and steadied her. Sara rose unsteadily to her feet. With Honey's help, Audrey helped guide her over to the bed.

"Thank you, Audrey," Sara whispered with a faint smile.

She blinked several times, her vision blurring as Audrey pulled the throw over her and tucked her in. She reached up and grasped Audrey's arm. Her lips parted and she tried to force out the words, but it seemed like she couldn't remember how to form them. Audrey held her hand tightly for a moment before she tucked it under the covers.

"Rest, Sara. I'm going to go check on Emma. If you can, let Jaguin help you fight your demons," Audrey whispered, smoothing her hair back from her face.

"Dragon," Sara finally mumbled, her eyes growing heavy. "I have a dragon. I... am... a dragon."

"I know," Audrey whispered. "and a dragon can conquer any demon, Sara, even the ones in your nightmares."

A soft smile curved Sara's lips as she sank deeper into the dark abyss. For the first time since her captivity, she wasn't afraid of it. She didn't know if it was because of the drug Audrey had given her or the knowledge that she had her own personal dragon.

Not one dragon, the soft, feminine voice in her head said. *You have two dragons. Our mate protect us, too. We not alone.*

No, I... we are not alone, Sara thought faintly as the shadow of a large silver dragon suddenly appeared next to the small brushed nickel colored one. *Oh, Jaguin, she is so beautiful.*

I know, my elila, Jaguin's voice caressed her. *Sleep. Let us watch over you.*

Sara released a sigh and rolled over onto her side. She felt the warmth of Honey as the symbiot jumped up onto the bed next to her. She was surrounded on all sides.

Thank you, Sara whispered before she released her hold on consciousness.

"I will always protect you, my brave mate," Jaguin murmured from the doorway of the bedroom.

Chapter 18

Two days later, Sara walked quietly across the room and sank down in the chair across from Emma. They sat in silence for several minutes before Sara sighed loudly and reached for the fragile young girl's hand. She bowed her head and drew in a deep breath. She and Emma had been through something no one should ever have to go through, but that did not change what had happened. They could not change the past; they could only control the present and focus on the future, wherever it took them.

Sara knew deep down that she had to take control of her present, because she wanted a future. She wanted a chance to live again, to find out who she was and what she was capable of. Over the last two days, she and her new dragon self had grown stronger. When she had finally woken, it was to find Jaguin sitting on the bed beside her – waiting patiently for her to wake up.

She closed her eyes and clutched the memory of his presence to her. She needed it to have the strength to complete the task she had set in motion. Fear threatened to choke her. Uncertainty about her decision clutched at her heart and throat with a greedy claw before she felt certainty settle over her, again. She knew she wasn't alone now, and never would be again.

"I'm going away for a little while, Emma," Sara said reluctantly, looking across at the pale features of the other woman. "I've been invited to go up into the mountains where there are some very unusual plants. I... I miss my research. I need to find a place for myself on this world and this is the one thing I know I'm good at," Sara began, unable to keep the tears from escaping as a wave of guilt swept over her. Her voice broke when Emma raised her hand and gently wiped the tear that escaped from her cheek. "You have to fight back, Emma. This is a good place to live even if it is different. The people here are... The people here are strange but they would never hurt us. Not like Cuello did. You have to fight back. I can't stand watching you fade away any longer. I... I need to heal and I can't do that unless I get back to doing what I love," she finished in an emotion-choked voice.

"Go, Sara," Emma whispered with a ghost of a smile. "I'll be alright. I promise."

Sara stared into Emma's eyes, frowning for a moment when she saw something glimmering deep in the other woman's eyes. There was a new awareness that she hadn't noticed before. There was also a swirl of color deep in the vivid blue eyes that Sara didn't remember seeing before – it was as if there was something alive inside Emma, something that the other woman may not even know was there.

Sara leaned forward and hugged Emma tight. It took a few seconds, but Emma's arms lifted and she wrapped them around Sara. They sat there for several long minutes before Sara reluctantly pulled away.

"I'll be back to check on you," Sara promised with a sniff. "Carmen and Creon also promised that they would take care of you and make sure that you are safe."

Sara watched as Emma nodded. Rising out of the seat, she bent and gave Emma one last kiss on the cheek before she turned and walked away. Only when she stepped out into the hallway and into Jaguin's arms did she let the tears fall.

"She will be fine," Jaguin promised. "Creon and Carmen have sworn they will do everything in their power to make sure that she is safe. She will heal. Creon will make arrangements for her to return to Earth if necessary."

Sara nodded and wiped her cheeks. "She has family there. Her mom, I think," she whispered. "I'm ready to go. Are you sure it is okay for you to leave?"

Jaguin nodded. "My services are not needed at the moment," he assured her. "If the royal family have need of my skills, they know where I will be."

A trembling smile curved Sara's lips. "So, besides being a warrior, what other type of skills do you have?" She asked in a somewhat breathless voice.

Jaguin's eyes glittered with mischief. "I am one of the best trackers on Valdier...," he began.

"And... what else?" Sara asked, stepping closer to him and running her hands up his chest.

"The best lover that you will ever have," Jaguin proclaimed with a wicked smile before he bent and captured her lips in a hard, passionate kiss that promised he would prove his claim.

"I can't wait for you to show me," Sara replied huskily.

* * *

Sara's words echoed in Jaguin's mind. It didn't help that he couldn't keep his eyes off of her. He grunted when she handed him the last basket that she had grabbed. He grimaced and sent a mental command to Honey that they were going to need a slightly bigger transport.

"It's your fault – and Honey's," Sara muttered as she picked up a smaller case. "I told you that you were giving me loads of stuffed sloths."

Jaguin glanced back at the back of the transport. It was filled to overflowing with the stuffed creatures. Arms, legs, and heads stuck out everywhere. Huge, rounded eyes, some wide, others half lidded as if the creatures were sleepy, stared back at him.

"I did not realize that Honey was bringing them to you as well until it was too late," Jaguin defended with a crooked smile. "Luckily, we were able to fit them all on the transport."

Sara chuckled as she climbed into the elegant interior. She couldn't help but release a soft whistle when she saw the bucket seats formed out of gold. Even though she knew what Honey could do, the symbiot continued to amaze her.

"This is incredible," Sara said, climbing into the seat on the right. "Is there anything it can't change into?"

Jaguin thought for a moment before he shook his head. "No, not that I know of," he replied.

"How fast can Honey go?" Sara asked.

Jaguin watched as Sara ran a caressing hand along the arm of the golden seat. A soft groan threatened to escape him. While the symbiot might look like a space ship, it was still his symbiot. Every touch, every caress that Sara made to the gold body of the ship felt like she was caressing him. For all its physical appearance, it was still connected to him.

"Sara," Jaguin muttered before he shook his head. "Fast enough when necessary. Take us home, my friend," he instructed, settling into the seat next to Sara.

But take your time, he added silently.

It had been almost three days since he had joined with Sara; his body and his dragon were begging for a repeat. If he was lucky, he might convince Sara of that as well. After all, what better way to pass the time on a weary trip?

"This is exciting," Sara said, leaning forward so she could look out of the front screen. "How does it do this?" She asked, glancing at him briefly before returning her gaze to the front. "It looks like glass, but I know that it isn't."

"It is able to reflect the environment around it," Jaguin explained, counting the seconds until they were far enough from the palace that he could distract her.

"How long will it take us to get to your village?" Sara asked.

Jaguin glanced out the window. They had just passed over the edge of the cliff and were heading down along the coast. In another twenty minutes, they would begin the turn inland toward the forests where he had taken Sara just a few short nights ago.

Sweat began to bead on his brow as he remembered the intense pleasure. Jaguin finally released a strangled curse. He was about to rise out of his seat when Sara pinned him to it, wrapping around him, her lips clinging to his while her hands worked frantically at the fastenings of his shirt.

"You have far too many clothes on," she groaned, leaning back and pulling her shirt up over her head.

"Goddess, Sara!" Jaguin exclaimed before she sat up just far enough to thrust one taut nipple into his mouth.

"That's it, suck it," Sara groaned, her hand moving over his shoulders under the material. "The other one. You can't forget it."

Jaguin's hands worked to release her trousers while his mouth, tongue, and teeth teased her nipples. He was happy that she had already discarded her shoes. He was going to have to seriously think of different footwear, something easy to kick off. He clumsily worked at toeing first one, then the other boot off. At least they were shorter boots and didn't require unstrapping.

His eyes widened as an idea came to him, but he quickly discarded it. With Sara's past, there was no way that she would allow him to strap her down. The thought disappeared when he gripped the side of her pants and pulled them down to her knees.

She rose up as high as she could on his lap without getting off. A smile tugged at her lips when he groaned. Sara leaned forward and gave him a hot, open-mouth kiss.

"Have you ever had a lap dance?" She asked in a husky voice.

Jaguin's throat worked up and down and he shook his head. The smile on her lips grew and she slid off his lap so she could kick her jeans off. His eyes moved to the material covering her womanhood. He licked his lips before raising his gaze to meet hers.

"I've never done this before either, but it might be fun," Sara said with a nervous smile. "Can you do me a favor and remove the rest of your clothes?"

"What will you do if I take them off?" Jaguin demanded.

"I'll give you a show you won't forget – or regret," Sara promised, lifting her hands to her breasts and cupping them before she slid them down her body and teased the material at her hips. "And you won't be destroying my panties. It took a while to get these made."

Jaguin licked his lips and nodded. "I don't wear any," he stated, standing up and pushing his trousers down.

"I... know," Sara choked out, her eyes glued to where his cock throbbed and bobbed up and down. "And might I say it would be a perfectly good waste of material if you did."

Jaguin chuckled and sat back down. He waved his hand in a circle. Sara, understanding that he wanted her to turn around, decided that if she was going to do it, she would do it in style. Pivoting on her heel, she struck a pose, one arm up, the other on her left butt check and her ass sticking out. The move thrust her breasts upward and made her think of what it felt like to ride him.

Moving slowly, Sara slowly pushed her panties down, taking tiny steps toward him as she did. When she was almost to him, she did a slow-motion twist and moved in a swaying arch toward him.

She thought she would have more time to tease and play with him, but the second that she was within reach, Jaguin had her by the waist and spun them both around. One minute he had been in the chair, watching her; the next, she was bent over it and he was pressed behind her. Sara's heart raced when she felt him nestled between her buttocks.

"Jaguin," she whispered in a trembling breath.

"Bend over, Sara," Jaguin demanded. "Place your hands down on the grips."

Sara looked down, stunned to see that two grips had formed on the back of the curved chair. She gasped when she felt him reach down and caress her hot, dripping curls. She had gone from moist to ready in three seconds flat once she had started her little tease session.

"I've never..." Sara started to say, when she felt his hand slide up and then spread her. "Jaguin." She moaned, bowing her head.

"So beautiful," Jaguin whispered, aligning his cock with her tight entrance. "Do you trust me, Sara?"

Sara's breath caught when she felt the tip of his cock pressing against her. She nodded, waiting for him to continue. A shiver ran through her when she felt his fingers caress the faint scars that crisscrossed her back. She had to bite her lip to keep from crying out.

"Tell me, Sara. Do you trust me?" Jaguin asked again in a quiet, soothing voice.

"Yes," She whispered. "Yes, I... trust you, Jaguin."

"As I trust you, my mate," Jaguin replied, pressing forward.

Sara gasped and breathed deeply. From this angle, he filled her until she wasn't sure she could take any more. She bent forward and spread her legs further. He pushed deeper into her vaginal canal from behind, and it left her feeling vulnerable and exposed. A whimper escaped her when he gripped her hips tightly between his hands and began rocking her back and forth so she was the one impaling him.

"That is it, my *elila*. You have the power to take me," Jaguin swore, watching as his cock disappeared into her over and over. "How much can you take, Sara? How much of me are you willing to claim as yours?"

Fire built inside Sara. She looked over her shoulder at him. His face was taut with desire. The muscle in his jaw twitched as he tried to hold on to his control. Suddenly, Sara wanted to be the one to break through that control. Holding onto the grips,

Sara rocked harder and faster, taking him deeper and deeper until she could feel him touching her womb.

Her breasts rocked with her. Every time she pressed forward, her nipples brushed against the living metal. As if he read her thoughts, Sara suddenly felt a tight squeeze on them. Thin ribbons of gold chain wound around each one, pulling and tugging with every move she made. A low cry escaped her when his right hand moved to her ass and he squeezed it. The added pressure was just enough to send her over the edge. She slammed back against him, burying him as far as she could take him, and she came hard, her vaginal canal fisting him as she pulsed.

"Sweet Goddess of the Hive," Jaguin groaned as his cock jerked deep inside Sara. His loud hiss filled the air as he fought to pull in air. "Sara!" He groaned again, his hips jerking in time with his pulsing release.

"I love you, my *elila*," he gasped, falling forward to cage her under his body. "I love you so much, Sara."

Sara bowed her head; tears burned her eyes from the intensity of the feeling ricocheting through her. His words were like a soothing balm to her shattered soul. She wasn't ready to say the words out loud yet, but she knew deep in her heart that she loved him, too. She loved Jaguin more than life itself. Without him, she wouldn't know what life truly was.

* * *

Sara groaned and stretched. She froze when she realized that it felt like they were no longer moving. Her head turned and her eyes widened when she also realized that they were no longer alone. A soft cry escaped her and Sara pulled the golden sheet covering her up to her chin.

"Jaguin," Sara whispered, nudging Jaguin with her foot. "Jaguin, wake up!" She hissed when all he did was groan and roll over.

Unfortunately, when he rolled, Honey didn't go with him, or at least, Honey the sheet didn't go with him. Sara's face flamed when the huge male staring at them released a sigh and shook his head.

"Jaguin," the man said sharply.

Jaguin might not have woken for her, but he did when he heard the man's voice. In a flash, he was on his feet, a long knife that Sara didn't remember him having clutched tightly in his fist. Sara's blush deepened when an older woman peeked her head inside and grimaced.

"Jaguin, put some clothing on," the woman ordered. "I saw enough of your bare body when you were a lad, I have no desire to see it as a full grown male. Your father is more than enough for my poor eyes."

"Yes, mother," Jaguin muttered, reaching for the blanket Sara was clutching to her chest.

"Oh, no, you don't," Sara snapped. "Find your own blanket. This one is mine."

"I wouldn't mind seeing her," a younger male said.

"Get out of here, Jaire," Jaguin growled, reaching for his clothing.

Sara stared back at the young boy. He looked like a younger version of Jaguin. She blinked when he suddenly grinned at her. Even his smile looked like Jaguin. Doubt and confusion filled her when she glanced back at the older man.

"Boy, back up. Let your brother and his mate get dressed," the man ordered.

"Yes, sir," Jaire muttered, winking at Sara before he stepped backwards out of Honey.

Sara turned her head to stare at Jaguin. He could feel the flush rising in his cheeks at her raised eyebrow. Bending, he picked up his shirt and pulled it on, not bothering to fasten the hooks in the front.

"Please tell me I didn't just meet your family while we were both naked," Sara asked in a trembling voice.

Jaguin grinned. Sara, recognizing that she had definitely just met his family, groaned and buried her face against her knees. She wished the ground would just open up and swallow her. Why, oh why, did life have to be so unfair at times? Hadn't hers been screwed up enough without adding 'meeting the in-laws while in the buff' to the list?

"Sara," Jaguin murmured, sliding his hands along her bent head and threading his fingers in her hair. "Look at me."

"Go away. I just want to die in peace," she mumbled.

A deep sigh escaped Jaguin. "Sara, *elila*, look at me," he coaxed. "Please."

"I'm dying here of total embarrassment," Sara stated in a muffled voice. "Go away."

"They will love you," Jaguin whispered tenderly.

Sara lifted her head and glared at him. "They probably think I'm some super slut you picked up at a bar somewhere," she sniffed, wiping at the angry tears.

"Never," he swore. "They know you are my mate. They see the way my symbiot is wrapped around you. It would never do that for anyone who was not my mate."

"How can you be sure?" Sara demanded, looking at him suspiciously.

"You are covered in the marks of my dragon," Jaguin pointed out.

Sara looked down at the faint mark of a dragon on her arm. Her gaze reluctantly moved to her right shoulder. She had one there as well. Lifting her left arm, she noticed one on the inside of her wrist. She really *was* covered with the marks.

"When did I get that one?" She asked, holding up her wrist.

"I believe that one is new," Jaguin chuckled. "As is the one on the inside of your left thigh."

Sara stared at him in disbelief before she lifted the blanket to check. Sure enough, there was a mark on her thigh. How in the hell did she not remember him biting her there? She dropped the blanket and glared at him.

"I'm going to muzzle you if you don't quit biting me," she snapped.

Jaguin chuckled and brushed a kiss across her pouty lips. "Wait until you see your breasts. My dragon really does want to see his mate," he murmured before he captured her lips in a heated kiss.

Sara's soft moan died in her throat. Her hands rose to tangle in his hair. Another moan rose when her nipples, sensitive from their earlier lovemaking, brushed against the soft material of his shirt. They immediately tightened into taut peaks.

"Wow! You really did claim her as your true mate!" A voice behind them exclaimed in awe, pulling them both back to the present with a resounding crash.

"Is he really your brother?" Sara asked, shivering as Jaguin wrapped his arms around her in order to give her a little modest coverage.

"Unfortunately, yes," Jaguin gritted out before he smiled. "But, I am soon to become an only child once again," he snapped out, adding the last part in a loud voice.

"I'm leaving," Jaire complained. "Mother said dinner will be served soon and not to get too distracted."

"Then, I suggest you get out of here so that Sara can get ready," Jaguin ordered. "Honey, seal the transport."

Sara buried her face in Jaguin's chest when Honey suddenly pitched and rolled, sending Jaguin's young brother flying backwards before the entrance to the ship closed, sealing them blissfully inside. Sara giggled when she heard the muffled curse followed by a repeat not to keep their mother waiting.

"I'm hungry!" Jaire yelled.

"He is always hungry," Jaguin replied dryly, sliding off the bed and standing. "Come, he will not go away until we come out."

"How do you know?" Sara asked, turning to slide her legs over the side.

Jaguin grinned when the golden bed suddenly rose, gently pushing Sara to her feet. He wrapped his arms around her, enjoying the feel of her naked body in his arms. His gaze softened when he saw her startled look.

"Because I wouldn't have when I was his age," Jaguin replied, grimacing when he heard Jaire yell again for them to hurry up. "Come, I will help you get dressed."

Chapter 19

Sara laughed and smiled at Cheri. Jaguin's mother had welcomed her into the family with a huge hug and a warm heart.

Sara had been so afraid that Jaguin's parents would not accept her. After all, she was different from any of the other women on the planet. She was the alien.

Instead of feeling awkward, Cheri had taken her under her wing, showing her around the bustling village, and introducing her to a host of residents. Sara was sure she would never remember everyone's name.

"Jaguin's dragon must be so happy to have found his mate at last," Cheri said, breaking into Sara's thoughts of her first few days in the remote mountain village.

"His dragon?" Sara repeated, turning from where she was storing some of the fresh produce they had just picked up at the market. "Yes, he is. I see him every day. He is so much calmer than he was!"

Cheri laughed and shook her head. "He should be," she replied with a twinkle in her eye. "Just remember, a male dragon likes a challenge. If he demands you submit, you twitch your tail – and slap him upside the head with it for thinking he can boss you around."

"My tail?" Sara repeated, this time in a quieter tone. "I... don't have a tail."

"You don't.... Oh, you poor child, I'm so sorry," Cheri murmured, turning to wrap her arms around Sara. "Jaguin will love you even if your dragon does not have a tail."

"No, no, it's – Well, I don't have a dragon either. I mean I do. I hear her in my head, but I've never... you know, actually turned into a dragon," Sara finally muttered.

A look of confusion, followed by clarity, swept across Cheri's face. She raised an eyebrow at Sara and placed her hands on her hips. Sara blushed and fidgeted with a jar of freshly made jam.

"Has Jaguin not shown you how to shift into your dragon yet?" Cheri asked with a knowing look.

Sara shook her head. "No, he said he didn't think I was ready yet. I know he is having difficulty controlling his dragon. He... He's worried that it might hurt me," she softly admitted.

"I need to have a talk with Jaguin's father," Cheri commented dryly. "It is obvious he has seriously neglected the education of his oldest son. I can only imagine what he has forgotten to tell Jaire."

Sara's lips twitched. "Jaire seems pretty smart," she reflected, thinking of the teenage boy.

Cheri sighed and shook her head. "Village talk among the younglings. He will get himself in trouble if he listens to them, you mark my words. Follow me," Cheri instructed, wiping her hands on a small towel before she turned and headed for the back door of the beautiful family home.

Sara quickly placed the jam on the counter and hurried after Cheri. She paused in the doorway leading out to the back gardens. As always, she stopped for a few seconds to absorb the beautiful, and bountiful, array of flora covering every square inch of the walled garden.

"What are we doing?" Sara asked, finally walking across the stone deck and descending the steps.

Cheri turned and smiled. "You are going to let your dragon out," Cheri stated with a happy clap of her hands.

"But, Jaguin said...," Sara started to argue before her voice faded at the disapproving look on Cheri's face.

"What Rolf should have explained to Jaguin, and I can only hope he remembers to tell Jaire, is that a male dragon will NEVER harm his mate." Sara watched as Cheri stepped up to her and clasped her hands firmly between her own. "Sara, it is the female dragon that rules the male. He is her protector, her companion, her partner, but *she* is his life. He could no more harm her than he could himself."

"Are you sure?" Sara asked, biting her lip as hope blossomed inside her.

"Positive. It is a knowledge passed down from mother to daughter," Cheri explained. "Only the females of the royal family have the power to shift into a dragon without the Dragon's Fire. They have a direct connection to the Hive, home of the Goddesses and the giver of the symbiots. The rest of the women must hope to find a true mate. Yet, the males need us even more than we need them. For we do not have to accept every part of them, not the way that the three parts of the male have to accept us. When we do, we hold the power of the future, for we give birth to the next line of dragons. You were given this gift by the Goddess. It is time my son's dragon knows his mate."

Sara nodded before Cheri even finished. Her lips parted when Cheri murmured for her to call to her dragon. Sara listened as Cheri told her what she needed to do.

"Call to her, give her your strength, and trust in her," Cheri instructed quietly. "She will be frightened the first time, especially without her mate here. I will guide you both. Do not be afraid of the change. Embrace it, accept it, and let the magic of the Goddess wash through you. You will still be there, just as your dragon is with you."

"Okay," Sara whispered, drawing in a deep breath and focusing inward. "Come to me."

My mate? Her dragon asked in a sleepy voice.

He isn't here. I need you to come take over. I need to learn how to let you out, Sara said.

No, my mate call me. I come when he call, her dragon said stubbornly.

Jaguin's afraid to let him call you. We have to show him that his dragon won't hurt you, Sara explained. *Please, trust me. Cheri is here. She'll guide you.*

I no want to, her dragon whimpered. *I wait for him.*

"Come to me, child. I wish see my new daughter," Cheri's firm voice demanded. "Come!"

Sara gasped when she felt her dragon's response to the deeper voice of the older dragon. Cheri had partially shifted.

Everything blurred for a moment before things became clear. Sara drew in a hissing breath. Things weren't just clear, they were brilliantly sharp. She could actually see the small hair-like texture on a nearby leaf that would have required a magnifying glass to see before.

Turning, she lost her balance when she tripped over her tail. Sara blinked and stared in disbelief. She had a tail – and wings.

I a dragon, her dragon crowed in delight. *I free.*

Yes, you are and a very lovely one at that, Cheri stated, using her head to help Sara stand up again. *Now, you must watch your tail. It is a very useful tool, but can be a bit of a nuisance if you are not careful.*

How can it be a..., Sara started to ask at the same time as her tail swung around and shattered a small pot filled with tiny flowers. *Oh, sorry!*

Cheri chuckled. *If one small pot is all that will be lost, I believe we will be most lucky. Come, we need more room,* she decided.

For what? Sara asked, trying to follow behind Cheri without damaging anything else.

To fly, Cheri said.

To... fly?! Sara whispered, swallowing. *Hold on a minute. I don't know the first thing about flying. I've been up in a plane and I've ridden Jaguin's dragon and that is about the extent of my knowledge.*

Cheri turned and looked at Sara. Her tail swung around and she used the tip to lift the young dragon's chin so that she was forced to look at her and not the ground. Sara swallowed when she saw the beautiful silver and white dragon staring back at her.

You may not know anything about flying, Sara, but your dragon does. She was born with the instinct bred over millions of years. Release her, become her, and you have nothing to fear, Cheri said in a quiet, soothing voice.

Sara thought of what Cheri was telling her. She knew it was true in both plants and animals. Plants had evolved over millions of years, changing and adapting to their environment, like the huge Sequoias in California who needed fire to survive. Without fire, the cones they dropped would never open, releasing the seeds. Sara knew about thousands of plants that needed a wide range of things to live and thrive. Animals had done the same thing. The knowledge was passed down through the genetics from one generation to the next.

Can you fly? Sara asked her dragon.

Yes, I fly. I know how to fly, her dragon respond with glee. *I fly. You see.*

Okay, show me, Sara ordered.

It easy, just flap wings, her dragon stated.

Just... Sara started to repeat in disbelief when she clamped her lips tightly together.

She could feel the rumble of her dragon laughing at her. Sara snorted – *just flap your wings. Smart, real smart. My dragon has a sense of humor.*

Brilliant, Cheri chuckled.

Sara ignored both of them when she felt the muscles in her dragon tighten. One minute she was on the ground, the next she was soaring upward over the trees. Her breath caught in awe at the feeling of power washing over her. She felt –

Free, her dragon whispered. *We are free.*

Tears burned Sara's eyes. Yes, they were free. Audrey was right. There was nothing more powerful than a dragon, not even Cuello or his men. Sara released the last tiny bit of restraint she held over her dragon, giving the beautiful creature complete control.

The joy that swept through the dragon took her breath away. She and Cheri flew through the clouds, playing hide and seek among the fluffy white puffs of moisture. Sara's wings sparkled like diamonds where the droplets pooled. Not to be outdone, Cheri turned and folded her wings. Together, they spiraled downward, opening their wings mere feet from the tops of the trees. They glided over the tops of the high grass in the meadows and reached down to snare fish from the river, tossing them into the air and eating them before they could disappear.

For the next two hours, Sara learned what it meant and felt like to be a dragon. Cheri showed her how to land on the high branches of a tree and how to drink the water captured in the huge stems of a red bloom. Cheri also explained what the different plants were and how they used them for different things.

"This knowledge is usually passed down from father to son, and from mother to daughter. You are one of us now. My daughter," Cheri said, tucking a strand of Sara's hair behind her ear.

Sara gave Cheri a grateful, delighted smile and hugged Jaguin's mother close, her heart still pounding from the thrill of discovery. "Today was incredible, Cheri. Thank you," she said as she drew back.

"You can thank me by giving my son and his dragon the peace of having his true mate in every way," Cheri murmured, cupping Sara's cheeks. "And giving me a few grand-younglings to play with wouldn't hurt either."

Sara blushed and laughed. "Let me get the first part down before I think about the second part. Something tells me that my dragon needs a little more time to get used to me as much as I need to get used to her. I would like to learn how to be a dragon before I show Jaguin," she chuckled. "Where are the guys?"

"I think that is a very good idea. Male dragons can be a bit – demanding at first," Cheri laughed. "Rolf and Jaguin have taken Jaire out hunting – again," Cheri continued, stepping back and walking toward the house. "If I know Jaire, he has already abandoned the other two and gone off to join some of his friends."

Several minutes later, Sara laughed when the two men returned without Jaire who had disappeared shortly after they left. Rolf threatened to ground the young boy. He growled and threatened every form of torture a parent could think of until Cheri pulled out a fresh pie that she had just removed from the oven.

"The boy has to learn to control his curiosity," Rolf grumbled between bites of the still hot pie. "It's going to get him in trouble if he doesn't."

"I know," Cheri responded with a twinkle in her eye. "Just like it got Jaguin in trouble when he was younger."

Jaguin's soft groan and muttered warning sent Sara into a fit of giggles. She was still soaring high from her experience earlier in the day. Resting her chin on the palm of her hand, she leaned forward and winked at Cheri.

"These totally sounds like blackmail stories," Sara said with a huge grin. "You wouldn't happen to have any photographs, I mean images, of those times would you?"

"Of course," Rolf replied immediately. "I'll put them on in the other room."

"Father, no!!!!" Jaguin groaned, pushing back his chair and rising to try to intersect his father. "I thought I destroyed all of those!"

"I made copies, a lot of them. You boys think I don't know that you would try to destroy them?" Rolf was saying when Sara and Cheri walked into the other room.

"I deny it all," Jaguin growled under his breath.

"I'm sure you do," Sara whispered back, running her hand along his jaw. Her gaze softened when she looked up and saw the glitter of amusement dancing in his eyes. "Thank you," she said, suddenly serious.

"For what?" Jaguin asked, tilting his head and gazing down at her.

Sara slid her hands up over his shoulder and held herself steady. "For showing me what it is like to have a real family," she replied, brushing her lips across his.

Jaguin held her for several long seconds, uncaring that his father and mother were arguing about which vidcom went first. He held Sara close to his heart. For a brief second, he wished that he could return to Earth and show Sara's mother and aunt what they were missing out on – for a brief second. Then, he let it go. Even if he could, he seriously doubted that they could comprehend the amazing woman that Sara had become.

"One day, we will have a family of our own," Jaguin murmured in her ear.

"We already do," Sara replied, thinking of his mother, father, and brother. "We have each other."

"Do I have to claim Jaire?" Jaguin asked playfully.

Sara laughed when a younger version of Jaguin suddenly appeared on the screen. She had to look twice to make sure it wasn't Jaire. Jaguin grimaced when she raised her eyebrow at him.

"All the girls loved the dragon races," Jaguin muttered, wincing when he saw the way he was strutting around.

"You look like a rooster, strutting his stuff," Sara commented, sliding down onto the long couch to watch the vidcom.

Jaguin started to ask what a rooster was when Honey sent him an image from Sara. He muttered a soft curse and sank down next to her. Leaning over, he couldn't resist whispering in her ear.

"Oh, really?" Sara muttered, raising her eyebrow at him. "I'd like to see your tail do that."

Chapter 20

Several days later, Jaguin froze, his gaze locked on his prey. He hadn't planned on hunting this particular delicacy, but the tantalizing scent had been too much for his dragon. Jaguin realized that now that he had let his dragon out, there was no way he was going to be able to harness him again. All he could do was hope that his dragon would stay calm and rational.

That hope went out the window when he felt his body slowly stretch out and balance on the thick branch of the tree. If the damn thing hadn't been driving him nuts to get out, he would have never been in this predicament.

Careful, my friend, the branches are damp from the dew, Jaguin cautioned, hoping his dragon would want to shift to prevent the possibility of falling.

He smothered the grin that threatened to escape when his dragon released a puff of hot air at the insult. Jaguin quickly squelched the hope of tricking his dragon back into compliance. No, his dragon was focused on one thing and one thing only – the prey he was determined to catch this morning.

We need to find the right time to call forth her dragon, Jaguin insisted. *We agreed earlier that if I let you out, you would tire yourself out today so that when we call her dragon, you won't just jump her.*

She not mind me jump her. She like me better. She no get mad if I jump her, his dragon snorted.

But what if you hurt her? Jaguin asked quietly.

You no hurt her, I no hurt her, his dragon insisted.

Jaguin would have argued that fact if it hadn't been the truth. His gaze softened on the slender figure stepping carefully through the tall ferns. He had followed her everywhere over the last few days and somehow, she always seemed to know it, no matter how careful he was.

This time, though, he was in his dragon form. It was the first time he had shifted away from everyone. Before, he had stayed close to his father, knowing that the older dragon would help calm his own.

He refocused as he felt the muscles of his dragon stiffen when Sara stopped and looked around with a puzzled frown. There was no way she could know he was here. Absolutely, positively no way... until his front foot slipped on the slippery moss and he found himself hanging upside down from the tree branch by his tail.

"I knew you were here," Sara whispered with an exasperated sigh. "I've missed you. Jaguin really needs to let you out more often," she said, scratching him behind his ear.

Jaguin's dragon gave Sara a sharp-toothed grin and licked her cheek. Her soft chuckle washed through him and he could have been fine except she hit that magic spot he liked and his left paw started thumping. The moment it did, he lost his hold on the branch and crashed to the soft ground with a thud. Sitting up, Jaguin shook his head and snorted.

"Are you okay?" Sara murmured, reaching out to rub his head before giving him a quick kiss on the top of it. "I bet I know what will make that all better."

Jaguin's dragon purred and rubbed his head against her hand. Sara chuckled and stepped back to give him a coy look before she turned and walked back to where she had dropped the basket she was carrying. He really hoped it was some of the fresh wild berries that grew in the forest. He loved those. While she was checking on her basket, Jaguin turned his attention to his dragon.

You dropped me from that branch on purpose, he growled to his dragon.

She kiss head. I tell you I be good, his dragon responded.

Just behave yourself! Jaguin retorted.

You jealous, his dragon snorted. *Our mate like me. You no want to share.*

I do want to... Oh, Goddess give us strength, Jaguin muttered, staring back at where Sara had been checking on her basket.

In her place stood a petite dragon, holding a basket full of berries by her tail. Jaguin could feel his dragon's mouth water. He highly suspected it wasn't for the berries. That assessment proved correct when Sara used her tail to place the basket on a nearby stump. He might have had a chance of controlling his dragon – a very, very small, impossibly minuscule chance – if she had not turned around and bent over.

With her tail in the air, Jaguin murmured mesmerized.

Her tail in air! His dragon roared.

Dragon's balls, Jaguin groaned.

Yes, all the way to my balls, his dragon announced, nodding his head up and down fervently before he leaped over the tall ferns and landed behind Sara.

Jaguin was mortified when his dragon leaned forward and drew in a deep breath. The rich aroma of the female dragon's arousal slapped him in the face about the same time as her tail did. The male dragon sat down in stunned disbelief. Shaking his head, he released a soft snarl.

Mine! He growled.

The female dragon snorted and ran the tip of her tail up along his jaw before tapping his chin. The male, unsure of what she was doing, felt his jaw drop when her tail weaved back and forth down his chest to his…

Did she just? I… Hot Mother of Lava, Jaguin choked out when he felt the tip of Sara's tail wrap around his dragon's cock. *You'd better hope she doesn't decide to slap that, my friend, or neither one of us is going to be doing anything but eating mud.*

She… no… she… no, his dragon kept repeating as Sara's tail moved up and down the growing length of him.

Sara, be careful, Jaguin warned. *A male dragon is built different from our two-legged form.*

I'm not doing this, Sara hissed back. *This hussy has her own agenda. She is NOT listening to me.*

Jaguin's chuckle echoed through both of them. *I think she wants him as much as he wants her. I guess I shouldn't have worried about whether she could handle it or not.*

Handle it? Do you have any idea how strange this feels? Sara demanded, hissing when she felt her dragon snap at the male's neck. *She's... Oh, my, goodness... I didn't know dragons had such long....*

Well, yes, they need them that long, Jaguin interrupted. *I think it is time to let them be together.*

Oh my, Sara whispered, fading into the background with a shudder.

'Oh my' is right, Jaguin muttered when he felt the muscles in his dragon tense. *This is about to get hot.*

Mine, the male dragon growled when he felt the tip of the female's tail running up the length of his engorged cock. Unable to completely pull it back into the protective slit, he knew he would need to mount the female before she got too far away. He reached out to sink his teeth into her hind quarters, but she turned and snapped at him, forcing him to jerk back.

This time, his roar shook the trees. The female, unconcerned by his show of strength and his demand for obedience, turned and lifted off the ground. The male rose up on his hindquarters and stretched his neck. His teeth sank into her tail, catching her in mid-flight. The female fought, struggling to free her tail by whipping it back and forth. Afraid he might hurt her, the male released her.

With a loud grunt, he forced his throbbing cock back into the slit. Surging upward, the male took to the sky after the female. He turned, slicing through a thin spot in the canopy. He paused for a moment, searching the sky for the female. A movement just above the treetops caught his attention. Twisting, he folded his wings and plunged downward.

The female, inexperienced in the art of battle, didn't see the male until it was too late. Startled, she let out a cry and tried to twist to the left to avoid being caught. The move left her underbelly vulnerable. She tried to correct her mistake, but lost her momentum and began to tumble back to the ground in an uncontrollable spiraling decent.

Sara's heart pounded and she urged her dragon to not panic. Deep inside, she braced for impact with the hard ground below. Twenty feet from the rocky riverbed, she suddenly felt her body gripped from above. Hope surged through her when the male wrapped his front and back legs around her and began pumping his wings frantically.

Sara could feel the water from the river slide along her back as she slid across the surface before her body began to rise again. A short distance from the river was a grassy bed, soft from years of runoff and build-up from the silt. It offered an island among the rocks.

The female dragon's heart still raced with fear. She had come close to serious injury, possibly even death in her desire to lead the male on a chase guaranteed to excite him. And boy had she excited him! The explosion of adrenaline that rushed through him fueled a singular, potent need to claim and protect the female he had wanted for centuries.

Jaguin set her down in the soft grass, still holding her firmly by her front and back legs. Sara's head fell back in sheer relief that she had survived, exposing her long, slender neck.

Jaguin struck hard and fierce, his fear turned to need, his anger to desire. His sharp teeth sank into the tender flesh of her neck. Breathing out the Dragon's Fire, he could smell the faint burning scent as it mixed with his mark. His cock, heavy and ready from before, was even fuller with the adrenaline still pulsing through his body.

He wrapped his tail around hers, pulling her up slightly and opening her for him. He continued to breathe his fire into her as he pulled back and then thrust forward in a primitive claiming of the male dragon to the female. Her soft, hoarse cry filled the air as the combination of the male and his fire branded her as his true mate.

A shudder ran through the male when he felt the tip of his cock catch and hold onto the female. Once he knew there was no escape for her, he lowered his wings, using the wing claws to lock with hers, and released her back legs so he could dig his into the soil. He did the same with his front claws, but kept his hold on her neck.

Locked together, he began moving, rocking back and forth in strong, powerful strokes, each one feeding on the Dragon's Fire burning through them. The hotter it burned, the faster he pumped until one orgasm faded into another in a primitive, ancient dance of joining. No longer were they two distinct entities, they were one; one heartbeat and one soul brought together by love.

It is not just the love between us, Sara whispered, feeling the connection of her dragon to the male.

No, a dragon's love is for eternity. There is only one true mate for them, born in the fire of the stars. Without it, they are lost, Jaguin replied as the male collapsed over the female, his wings wrapped tightly around her.

It is so beautiful, Jaguin, Sara murmured, loving the deep glow that had ignited inside her dragon.

I am glad you think so, Sara, because I think my dragon just gave you our first child, he said dryly.

What! How? Oh, she choked out, staring at the spark of light.

Well, first two dragons have to…, Jaguin teased.

It's so beautiful, Sara whispered, ignoring Jaguin as she caressed the tiny light.

Chapter 21

Sara carefully packed the last of the things they planned to take to the home that Jaguin had been working on. They had spent the last month with his parents and brother. She shook her head. It was hard to believe that time had flown by so quickly.

She and Jaguin were still awed by the closeness they'd felt since their dragons had come together that day almost a week ago. She blushed when she thought about it. Hell, between them and their dragons, it was amazing they had gotten anything completed at all. Their daily trips to their new home had turned into a 'catch me if you can' orgasm bonanza. She swore she was going to have to put her dragon on something if she didn't stop twitching her tail every time Sara let her out. It was like waving a red flag to the male.

"What happened?" Sara heard Cheri say anxiously from down the hall.

Sara stepped out of her and Jaguin's room in time to see Jaguin carrying Jaire's limp body into the room down the hall. She hurried forward, and stepped inside.

Dried blood ran from his nose and the corner of his mouth. Cheri frantically stripped his clothing off while his symbiot jumped up on the bed to lie over him. The moment the symbiot touched him, Jaire jerked and screamed in pain.

"What is it?" Rolf demanded, hurrying into the room. He took stock of Jaire's condition, and took a deep breath. "I've seen this before. Four other boys in the village have the same thing. Every time their symbiot tries to help them, they scream in pain and their symbiot retreats as if it is in pain as well."

Sara lifted her fist to her mouth to keep from crying out when Jaire's body began to jerk uncontrollably. Jaguin and Rolf hurried to each side to hold him down while Cheri cleared his airway.

"What are we going to do?" Cheri asked tearfully. "If his symbiot cannot heal him…."

"The village council has sent an urgent message to the palace asking them to send a healer," Rolf said in a grim voice.

"He won't make it," Cheri said, seeing the faint tint of blue beginning to form around Jaire's mouth and the fresh blood dripping from his nose. "He is dying."

Sara's eyes burned. She bowed her head and remembered her aunt saying the same thing years ago to the doctor. Vivid memories of Delilah resurfaced. She had been so young, just like Jaire, when she was lying still against the white sheets of her bed. Sara frowned when she saw something spilling out from under the shirt that Cheri had removed.

Stepping forward, she carefully picked up the shirt. A delicate yellow flower lay wilted on the floor. Sara stared at it with a frown. Something bothered her about the flower. She had seen or read something about it somewhere, but where?

Reaching up, she pulled one of the long hair pins out of her hair. She used the tip to turn the flower. As it turned, Sara observed the stem and the filaments. It was red, yellow, and black.

"Just like the snake," Sara murmured as her memories came back. "Morian said to never touch this flower, that it contained a poison that was deadly to not only the person who touched it, but to the symbiot."

"What?" Jaguin said, turning toward her.

Sara looked up, her face growing tight with concern. "The flower, it's poisonous. Morian Reykill, she had some in a special case in her atrium. She said the blossoms are so beautiful they are hard to resist, but when anything touches it, it injects poison into its victims. The poison is slow moving, but so toxic that it could even kill a symbiot if it received enough of it. I remember it because it reminded me of the Coral snakes back home. There was a saying 'Red on yellow, kill a fellow'. This has the red stem with the yellow petals. The filaments are black and they don't touch the petal," she explained in a fast, desperate tone.

"Is there an antidote?" Cheri asked in a pleading voice.

"Morian said she didn't know of any," Sara whispered, staring down at the flower.

"No!" Cheri's tortured cry filled the room.

"There has to be one," Jaguin growled, bending to pick up the flower.

"Don't," Sara warned, grabbing his wrist before he could. She looked at him, then at Rolf. "You have to warn the others in the village and ask if any of the other boys had a flower with them. Don't touch it. Use something to pick it up with, but keep it away from your skin."

"Surely there is some way to save our son," Rolf asked.

Sara bit her lip and looked back at Jaguin when he pulled his arm free. "Back home," she began, rising to her feet. "Back home, almost always where one poisonous plant lived, another plant that carried a cure for it grew nearby. It was always true in the woods where I lived and I found it to be true in my other studies."

"Do you know where Jaire was today?" Jaguin demanded.

His father nodded. "One of the boys was able to tell us before he collapsed. They were in the Hidden Falls cavern," Rolf responded.

"That would be about right. Morian had to keep these in a special box that remained dark except for a blue and red light," Sara said with a nod.

"Sara, do you think... Do you think that there might be a cure there?" Cheri asked in a husky voice.

Sara looked grimly back at Jaguin who nodded. "There's only one way to find out," she said, turning on her heel. "Jaguin, you know where the cave is, don't you?"

"Yes," he answered. "It will take us about twenty minutes by air to get there if we hurry."

"Let's go," Sara whispered, turning once more to look at Jaire. "I hope we can find it in time."

* * *

Sara had once asked Jaguin how fast Honey could go. She decided that she was glad that there was no speedometer attached to the symbiot by the time they landed ten minutes later. They had to have covered over two hundred miles.

"This way," Jaguin said, leading her up a steep trail. "There is the entrance."

Sara nodded and hurried forward. She paused at the entrance when Jaguin put his hand out and knelt. She waited as he searched the ground.

"Five prints, this one is Jaire's boot," he said.

"How do you know?" Sara asked, leaning down to look at the faint mark.

Jaguin stood up and gave her a grim smile. "Father cut a mark out of each of the left boots that Jaire owns. It makes it easier to track him," he told her.

"Smart man," Sara whispered.

Jaguin flashed her a smile. "Yes, he did the same with me when I was younger," he agreed, stepping into the cave.

Sara silently followed him. Her eyes scanned the dark interior. Light from the ceiling illuminated the interior of the cave. High overhead, Sara could see the glowing crystals that cast the eerie glow. Turning to look at Jaguin, she nodded toward the water.

"The flower is designed to collect water," she whispered. "Look near the water or any place that looks like water may drip down."

"I'll take the left side," Jaguin said.

It took them almost fifteen minutes to find the plants. They were hidden under a slight overhang. Once they located them, Sara searched the area near the outcrop. She cried out in relief when she found what she hoped they were looking for.

"Look at the colors," Sara said, pointing to the blossom.

"It is the same one," Jaguin stated with a frown.

"No, look. The blossom is red with a black stem. 'Red on black is a friend of Jack'," Sara murmured.

"Who is Jack?" Jaguin asked in frustration.

Sara shook her head. "Never mind. I know this is it," she said. "It has to be."

"How can we know for sure?" Jaguin asked.

Sara studied the flower for several long seconds. What if she was wrong? What if there was another plant that they had missed? Worse, what if the rules of nature back home didn't apply here? Once again, images of Delilah rose up in her mind and the doctor's insistence that he didn't need to listen to her aunt.

"We need to test it," Sara said, turning toward where the flowers the boys had picked rested.

Sara stopped when Jaguin's hand shot out and wrapped around her wrist. She stared up at him in surprise, then resignation. It was the only way to know.

"What do you think you are doing?" He asked in a deadly tone.

"I'm going to test it," Sara said, tugging on her wrist to free it. "It's the only way, Jaguin. You know that as well as I do."

Jaguin's head turned toward the overhang. "You can't," he said, turning away and walking over to the ledge.

"What are you doing?" Sara demanded, her heart racing. "Jaguin, don't!"

"What about our child, Sara? The poison would kill it, if not you," Jaguin said, staring back at her.

"If you die, I'm lost anyway," Sara whispered.

Jaguin bowed his head and was silent before he shook his head. "It is possible you could survive. You have a strong will to live. If you have our child, I know you will fight to survive for it," he said, turning back again.

"Jaguin, no!" Sara cried out, but it was too late.

As if in slow motion, she watched him reach over and pick one of the few remaining blooms. His fingers caressed the bloom. Then he turned back to Sara, a puzzled expression on his face.

"I feel fine," he said, staring back at her in confusion.

"It's a slow-acting poison," Sara said, taking a step forward. "and you are older and bigger than the boys."

They both looked down at the brilliant yellow flower with the red stem. Jaguin was about to touch it again when a drop of liquid fell onto the petal and slid down. Jaguin looked at Sara in confusion and saw the look of horror on her face. He reached up and touched the skin just under his nose. Pulling his fingers back, he noticed they were red with his blood.

"Sara," Jaguin started to say before the blossom fell from his fingers.

"Jaguin!" Sara cried out, reaching for him. She helped lower him to the floor of the cave.

"I guess it doesn't matter how big or old I am," Jaguin muttered, wincing as pain began to slice through him.

"This had better work," Sara said, carefully laying his head down on the smooth rock and scrambling to her feet.

She hurried over to where the other blooms were, plucked one, and ran back to where Jaguin lay moaning. She wasn't sure how to use the flower. Did it need to be processed to work?

"I don't know," she whispered in frustration. "I don't know how to make the antidote work."

Sara tried rubbing Jaguin's fingers in the center of the flower, but nothing happened. She sat down on the smooth rock and gently placed Jaguin's head onto her lap. She tenderly brushed his hair back from his face. She turned to study the bloom she was holding. How could it work? If just touching the other was enough to inject the poison, then surely…

"Drinking it," she murmured, noticing the red liquid in the bottom.

Sara didn't know what else to do. It was obvious that Jaguin was deteriorating. Sara tilted the petal until the liquid dropped into Jaguin's parted lips. She kept his head angled just far enough that he could swallow without choking. She waited and then poured a little more into his throat until she saw him swallowing.

It seemed like eternity before his eyelashes finally opened and he looked at her. A slow smile curved his lips. A trembling one curved Sara's in response.

"It worked," he said.

"You better be glad it did," Sara whispered before she burst into tears. "I am so going to beat you up for this when we get back."

"As long as it involves a little tail, I just might let you," Jaguin groaned as he sat up. "We need to get the antidote back to the village."

Sara nodded. She didn't want to destroy the plants, fearful if she did, they may never find any others. Instead, she had Honey form a small container and poured the liquid from each plant into it, then had Honey seal it.

"Let's go," Sara whispered, hurrying over the uneven ground back outside.

Chapter 22

Sara wiped the tears running down her face away. She stood in Jaguin's arms, her body shaking with emotion. Next to the bed, Rolf and Cheri held each other tightly, both crying.

"Jaguin," Jaire whispered above his mom's quiet sobs. "Jaguin."

"What, Jaire?" Jaguin growled, his own throat tight with emotion.

"Uh, did someone die or something?" Jaire asked, glancing nervously back and forth before he frowned down at himself. "Why am I naked?"

Jaguin and Sara's laughter warmed the room. Soon, Rolf joined in. Cheri was too busy swatting Jaire with the towel she had brought in to cool his face. After several starts and stops, Jaire explained that he and a few other boys from the village had gone to the cave to do some exploring. One of the other boys had found the pretty flowers and they all decided it would be a neat way to get the attention of the girls in the village. The boy had removed his shirt and used it to pick the flowers, afraid they would damage them. They didn't actually touch the flowers until they returned to the village and started to divide them up.

"I guess poisoning all the girls wouldn't make them too impressed, huh?" Jaire asked with a crooked grin.

"No, it wouldn't have been a good idea," Jaguin agreed. "They like Dragon Races better than flowers anyway."

"How would you know?" Sara asked with a raised eyebrow.

Jaguin's face flushed and he gave Sara a crooked grin that reminded her so much of Jaire that she had to resist rolling her eyes at the two of them. With a shake of her head, she decided that maybe she didn't want to know. After all, it wasn't as though he was likely to do it now.

"How about I show you?" Jaguin suggested with a mischievous grin.

Sara's eyes narrowed in suspicion. "Do the dragon races involve racing other guy dragons or...."

"Not when we get older," Jaguin grinned, stepping toward her. "I'll give you to the count of ten."

Sara turned on her heel and took off for the back garden, squealing with excitement when she heard Jaguin roar.

"Ten!"

"That was not counting to ten," Sara yelled, shifting into her dragon.

I never said I was going to play by the rules, he said, surging forward on powerful wings. *I do know about this wonderful place down by the river, though.*

I love you, Jaguin, Sara whispered.

I know, Jaguin responded. *I love you more.*

How did you know? Sara demanded, slowing so that he could easily catch up with her.

Jaguin swooped down from above and wrapped his arms and legs around her. *You talk a lot in your sleep.*

Sara's laughter filled the air as her mate carried her to the small island of grass near the river. Her wings rose to surround him. Both of them shifted at the last second, their arms and legs tangling as they clung to each other. Sara knew that her demons were gone once and for all, chased off by the dragon that had changed her life. He had done more than save her life; he had given her the home and the family she had thought would only ever be a dream.

* * *

Aikaterina stared into the pool of liquid that she had created. Her eyes softened on the two forms tangled around each other. She had returned from her travels just a short time ago. The small gold she had gifted to the two figures glowed brightly, as did the spark of life she could see cradled safely in the young human's womb.

"It is so nice to see the dragons find their mates," Arosa sighed, floating down to sit next to Aikaterina.

"Yes, it is," Aikaterina murmured, thinking of another set of dragons.

"Where did you go, Aikaterina? Did you find a new mate for one of the warriors?" Arilla asked curiously.

Aikaterina waved her hand over the pool. The image of the two lovers faded and she rose to walk along the river of gold. While the river looked wide, it was small in comparison to the vast universe. She stood looking down at the immature symbiots that were just beginning their life.

"I hope so," Aikaterina replied in a soft voice.

"What is wrong? You seem… sad," Arosa commented, staring in concern.

"Sad?" Aikaterina asked, tilting her head to the side and staring at Arosa.

"Yes. It is an emotion that I have felt from the human women," Arosa commented. "They are not sad now, but when they first came…." She stopped and looked at her sister for guidance.

"Is there anything we can do to help you?" Arilla asked hesitantly.

Aikaterina studied the two sisters. Her gaze traveled around the cavern they had created. The others that lived there were traveling through the vast star systems. Arosa and Arilla seldom left, preferring to remain close to the human women. Aikaterina raised her hand to her chest. She wondered what it would feel like to have a heartbeat, to feel… love.

"I have broken a law," she whispered, returning her gaze to the river of gold.

"You… You broke a law?" Arilla exclaimed in shock.

"Yes," Aikaterina replied.

"What law?" Arosa asked, stepping closer to Aikaterina.

Aikaterina turned and gave the sisters a slight smile. "The law to not interfere," she said. "There were two brothers, twins. They were the original Twin Dragons. I did not realize when I gifted their mother with two sons that it would be so difficult for them to find a mate."

"What did you do?" Arilla asked, reaching out to touch Aikaterina.

Aikaterina released a deep sigh and waved her hand. In front of them, a shimmering window appeared. Through it, two warriors stood gazing around in silence. She stared at them before waving her hand again. The window slowly faded.

"I gave them a second chance," she admitted, turning to step back to the shimmering pool of liquid. "I have given them thirty Earth days to find their mate."

"What happens if they don't?" Arosa asked quietly following Aikaterina back to the pool.

Aikaterina's smile faded. "Then, time will reset itself and they will die," she replied in a quiet voice. "It was all that I could give them."

"Why?" Arilla asked.

Aikaterina wearily sank down beside the pool. Her hand trembled as she waved it over the pool once again. Her eyes softened at the sight of the warrior holding the fragile yet incredibly strong female in his arms in their place by the river.

"It takes a great amount of energy to change the course of history," Aikaterina murmured, not looking up at Arilla.

"Arosa did it once," Arilla murmured, glancing at her sister.

"Yes, and it changed the course of the future," Aikaterina stated. "By changing the future for one, you will change the future for the other."

Arilla and Arosa looked at each other with a confused look. Aikaterina didn't miss the message that passed between the two sisters. She chuckled.

"You are both still very, very young. In time, you will understand what I mean. For now, just accept that for every action there is a reaction," Aikaterina said. "Leave me now, please. I must rest."

Arosa started to say something, but stopped when she saw her sister shake her head and float upward. They faded, watching in silence as Aikaterina observed the two figures lying in the grass near the river for several long minutes before she rose and walked over to the river of gold flowing through the Hive.

"Why do you think she is sad?" Arosa whispered to her sister, watching as Aikaterina sank down into the river.

"I don't know," Arilla replied.

Chapter 23

Sara glanced down at Jaguin's relaxed features. They had made love in both forms several times over the course of the afternoon. They had eventually fallen asleep, lured by the sound of the water, the gentle warm breeze, and exhaustion from their exuberant lovemaking.

Sara didn't know what woke her from her sound sleep. She was surprised when she realized it wasn't because of her nightmares. She blinked and sat up, shocked to find that she was wearing a loose gown made of blue silk.

"I thought you would be more comfortable if you were wearing clothes," a soft feminine voice said.

Sara started when she saw the figure of a woman sitting on a rock nearby. Her lips parted in surprise when Honey walked over to the woman and rubbed her head against the woman's leg. Sara blinked several times, wondering if she was hallucinating.

"Who... Who are you?" Sara asked in confusion.

"I am called many things, but here I am called Aikaterina," the woman replied.

"Jaguin...," Sara started to say, reaching her hand out to him.

"He sleeps," Aikaterina replied. "I wished to speak with you, Sara."

"Me?" Sara asked, pulling her hand back and touching the necklace around her neck. "Why? What about?"

"You were a wanderer on your world," Aikaterina murmured, smiling down at Honey. "I like the different names your species give my children."

"Your children?" Sara repeated, feeling like she was not only missing a few puzzle pieces, but the entire picture on the lid of it. "I'm sorry... I really don't understand who you are."

"Then let me show you," Aikaterina replied with a wave of her hand.

Sara stiffened and gasped as images burst through her mind. She saw a brilliant burst of light, then millions of galaxies forming. Her body twirled as the images rushed through her. Millions of planets and stars flashed by her, different species rose and faded, then everything came to a stop and she found herself standing in the cemetery back home.

"Where... Where are we?" Sara asked in a trembling voice, staring in growing panic at the familiar surroundings. "I know this place. I know this place," she repeated, taking a step toward the old oak tree. "I...."

Sara stopped and stared down at the small headstone. Fresh flowers decorated the grave. She blinked to clear her vision when the words became too blurry to see.

"Delilah," she whispered, lifting her head to stare back at Aikaterina. "Why? Why did you bring me here?"

"So that you could say goodbye," Aikaterina said, turning to gaze down at the grave. "Deep in your heart, you always wanted to come back and tell her goodbye."

"How… How did… How do you know that?" Sara demanded, growing angry.

"Is that not what you wanted?" Aikaterina asked.

"No," Sara said, turning away before she stopped and frowned. "Wait a minute!"

Sara turned back and stared back at the grave. "That's wrong," she said with a shake of her head.

"What is wrong?" Aikaterina asked, tilting her head to the side.

"The… The date of birth," Sara said, pointing to the headstone. "Delilah was born…."

Sara's voice faded when she saw the figure of a young woman walking toward her. Her eyes widened in shock and disbelief. It looked like Delilah! The woman was not the 10-year-old child Sara had known, but Sara would recognize Delilah's vivid hazel eyes and thick black hair anywhere. She shook her head. How was that possible?

"Delilah," Sara whispered.

"She cannot hear you," Aikaterina said, turning to look at the slender young woman walking toward them. "This is but a mirror to your world."

"A mirror? How is this possible? She died," Sara said, lifting a hand to wipe at her cheek.

Aikaterina was silent for a long time before she finally spoke. Her soft words washed over Sara, healing the wounds of pain and sadness that she had carried all through the years. Sara watched as Delilah stopped by the grave and knelt down to place a bouquet of flowers on it before she rose to brush some dirt off of the headstone. Amber Delilah Rosewater: Beloved wife and mother.

"Miss you, Momma," Delilah whispered. "Tell Daddy that I miss him, too. I'm doing good. I've found a lead on where Sara might be. I hope I can find her. I'm heading to a ranch in Wyoming next. It may take a while to find her, but I won't give up until I do."

"How can she be alive? I saw her die," Sara cried, turning to look at the figure beside her.

"When you change the course of time, it has a ripple effect on the rest of the universe," Aikaterina murmured.

"You... This is crazy! Are you telling me that you changed the course of time?!" Sara demanded, turning back to watch as Delilah continued to kneel by the grave. "She was dead!"

"Yes, she was," Aikaterina stated, turning to look at Sara.

Sara shook her head. "Why are you doing this?" Sara whispered. "Why?"

"Because without her, I could not correct a mistake I made," Aikaterina explained as she turned to stare at Delilah.

"What mistake?" Sara asked quietly.

Aikaterina turned to stare sadly at Sara. "Twin Dragons," she said.

"But, they have their mate," Sara said in exasperation. "Melina...."

"The original twin dragons," Aikaterina said. "The first ones – Barrack and Brogan."

"What does that have to do with Delilah?" Sara demanded in a soft voice.

Aikaterina turned to stare at Sara. "She is meant to be their true mate," she replied.

"You brought her back from the dead to be their true mate?" Sara asked in an incredulous tone.

Aikaterina softly chuckled. "I did not bring her back from the dead," she said with a twinkle in her eyes. "I turned back time. This changed the course of history. The ripple effect was meant to change the thread that ties the twin dragons. Delilah was part of that thread. As long as the thread remains unbroken, it will continue to exist."

Sara shook her head in confusion. "So, you're telling me that when you brought back the Twin Dragons, the first ones, that it somehow brought Delilah back as well?"

"Yes," Aikaterina said.

"And what happens if they don't find her and become her true mates?" Sara asked with a raised eyebrow.

"Then, time will reset itself and the history that was created for them will remain," Aikaterina replied in a solemn tone.

Sara drew in a deep, hissing breath. "Why are you showing me this? Why tell me all of this if she could still die?" She asked in a voice filled with pain.

Aikaterina watched the figure of Delilah as she walked back toward her car. She watched as the young human glanced back toward them, as if she was aware that she was being observed. A serene smile curved Aikaterina's lips. She could see the strength in Delilah's eyes.

"Because she will need you, Sara," Aikaterina replied, beginning to fade. "She will need your friendship."

"Wait! Aikaterina! You can't just leave," Sara snapped before she groaned. "Wait!"

"Sara," Jaguin's voice pulled at her.

Sara blinked several times to clear her vision. She stared up in confusion at Jaguin. She pushed against him and sat up, looking around wildly. She was back near the river. Turning, she stared at Jaguin.

"Where is she?" Sara asked in a choked voice.

"Where is who, Sara?" Jaguin asked, glancing around with a sharp gaze.

"Aikaterina," Sara asked, pushing up so that she could stand.

"Aikaterina?! Why... Where did you get that?" Jaguin asked, staring at the blue silk gown Sara was wearing. He glanced down at his body. He was dressed in the black uniform he normally wore when he was on duty. "When did I put this on?" He asked with a frown, turning to stare at Sara.

"Who is Aikaterina?" Sara asked in a trembling voice.

Jaguin ran his hands through his hair and frowned. "She is a Goddess of our people. It is said that our symbiots come from her blood. She gave us the gift of our dragon as a reward for saving her life. Why?"

Sara's lips trembled and she raised her hand to him. Warmth, love, and concern surrounded her at his touch. Stepping closer, she wound her arms around his waist and held him as tightly as she could.

"Because she gave me a chance to save an old friend," Sara whispered, leaning back to look up at his face. "I need to return to Earth."

"Earth!" Jaguin exclaimed in shock. "Sara...."

Sara saw the shock fade to awe as he stared over Sara's shoulder. She turned to see what had captured his attention. Stepping out of the woods were two huge warriors. A shiver ran through Sara when she saw the scars on them. These were not your typical warriors. These were...

"Twin Dragons," Jaguin hissed, pushing Sara behind him.

"Don't, Jaguin," Sara warned, grabbing his arm when his hand instinctively searched for the weapon at his side.

"Sara," Jaguin warned, never taking his eyes off the two warriors striding toward them.

"You are the one called Jaguin?" One of them called out.

"Yes," Jaguin replied in a loud voice. "Who are you?"

The men slowed to a stop almost a dozen feet away. They stared at Sara and Jaguin for several minutes before the one on the right rolled his shoulders and gave them a smile that didn't quite reach his eyes. Once again, Sara felt Jaguin stiffen.

"I am Barrack. This is my brother, Brogan," the man introduced. "We have need of a tracker."

"Why?" Jaguin asked in a sharp tone.

"To find our true mate," Brogan said.

"You have lost her?" Jaguin asked with a raised eyebrow.

Both men were silent again. "We have never found her," Barrack finally admitted.

Jaguin stared incredulously at them. "How do you expect me to find her if you don't even know who she is?" He asked.

Both men looked at each other before glancing at Sara. She stared back at them. Deep in their eyes, she saw a glimmer of desperation, sadness, and – acceptance.

"Her name is Delilah," Sara said quietly. "She is my best friend."

All three men stiffened. Hope flared in the two men's eyes as they stared back at her. Sara's hand went to the strange necklace she wore. Warmth filled her and she knew that she had made the right decision to speak up.

"Do you know where she is?" Barrack asked in a quiet voice.

Sara shook her head. "Not for sure," she admitted. "She is on my world. She said she was heading for a ranch in Wyoming. She is looking for me."

"Wyoming?" Jaguin said, turning partially to look at her. "Paul has a ranch in this place. We were at the ranch before I found you.'

"You will take us there," Brogan ordered.

"Please," Barrack added with a sharp glance at his brother. "Please, we do not have much time."

"Jaguin," Sara whispered, laying her hand on his arm. "They are telling the truth. They don't have much time, and neither does Delilah."

"Sara," Jaguin started to protest before he glanced at the two warriors. Turning back to Sara, he gazed deeply into her eyes. "You are sure?"

"Look into my mind," she whispered, staring up at him.

* * *

Jaguin stared into Sara's eyes and opened his mind. A soft hiss escaped him when he saw the images she was sharing. For a moment in time, he was standing beside Sara and the goddess. His gaze moved to the ethereal figure standing just a few feet from them.

"You are…," he started to say before he shook his head.

"Their time runs short warrior, as does the time of their mate. Help them," the figure replied. "Do not let them die in vain."

Jaguin stared back at the golden figure. There was a frailty about her that alarmed him and told him that she was growing weaker. His natural instinct to protect pulled at him to do what he could to help her.

"Guide them, warrior," the woman whispered. "That is how you may help me."

Jaguin nodded his head and held his hand to his chest. "With honor, my Goddess," Jaguin promised. "I will guide them."

"Thank you, Jaguin," Aikaterina whispered, fading.

"Jaguin," Sara's voice pulled him back to the present.

Jaguin turned to look at Sara before he focused on the two men. They both stood silently watching – waiting – for him to make his decision. A small rueful smile curved his lips and he wound his arm around Sara.

"We are going to need a ship," Jaguin said with a glimmer of determination in his eyes. "I think it is time I called in an old favor."

"Favor?" Barrack asked with a raised eyebrow.

"I hope you like the Curizans," Jaguin chuckled.

To be continued… **Twin Dragons' Destiny…**

If you loved this story by me (S. E. Smith) please leave a review. You can also take a look at additional books and sign up for my newsletter at **http://sesmithfl.com** and **http://sesmithya.com** to hear about my latest releases or keep in touch using the following links:

Website: http://sesmithfl.com
Newsletter: http://sesmithfl.com/?s=newsletter
Facebook: https://www.facebook.com/se.smith.5
Twitter: https://twitter.com/sesmithfl
Pinterest: http://www.pinterest.com/sesmithfl/
Blog: http://sesmithfl.com/blog/
Forum: http://www.sesmithromance.com/forum/

Additional Books by S. E. Smith

Short Stories / Novellas

For the Love of Tia (Dragon Lords of Valdier Book 4.1)

A Dragonling's Easter (Dragonlings of Valdier Book 1.1)

A Dragonlings' Haunted Halloween (Dragonlings of Valdier Book 1.2)

A Dragonling's Magical Christmas (Dragonlings of Valdier Book 1.3)

A Warrior's Heart (Marastin Dow Warriors Book 1.1)

Rescuing Mattie (Lords of Kassis: Book 3.1)

The Beast Prince (The Fairy Tale Series)

Science Fiction Romance / Paranormal Novels

Cosmos' Gateway Series
Tink's Neverland (Book 1)

Gracie's Touch (Book 1)
Krac's Firebrand (Book 2)

Paranormal / Time Travel Romance Novels

Spirit Pass Series
Indiana Wild (Book 1)
Spirit Warrior (Book 2)
Second Chance Series
Lily's Cowboys (Book 1)
Touching Rune (Book 2)

Science Fiction / Action Adventure Novels

Project Gliese 581G Series
Command Decision (Book 1)

Young Adult Novels

Breaking Free Series
Voyage of the Defiance (Book 1)
The Dust Series
Dust: Before and After (Book 1)

Recommended Reading Order Lists:
http://sesmithfl.com/reading-list-by-events/
http://sesmithfl.com/reading-list-by-series/

Excerpts of S. E. Smith Books

If you would like to read more S. E. Smith stories, she recommends Abducting Abby, the first in her Dragon Lords of Valdier Series. Or if you prefer a

Paranormal or Time Travel with a twist, you can check out <u>Lily's Cowboys</u> or <u>Indiana Wild</u>...

Audiobooks are also available. For a list of available audiobooks and to listen to samples visit: <u>http://sesmithfl.com/category/books/audio-books/</u>

About the Author

S.E. Smith is a *New York Times, USA TODAY, International, and Award-Winning* Bestselling author of science fiction, romance, fantasy, paranormal, and contemporary works for adults, young adults, and children. She enjoys writing a wide variety of genres that pull her readers into worlds that take them away.

CPSIA information can be obtained
at www.ICGtesting.com
Printed in the USA
LVHW051507051118
596010LV00013B/986/P